BARREN

BARREN

WITHDRAWN

Peter V. Brett

HARPER Voyager
An Imprint of HarperCollins*Publishers*

BARREN. Copyright © 2018 by Peter V. Brett. All rights reserved. Printed in the United States of America. No part of this book may be used or reproduced in any manner whatsoever without written permission except in the case of brief quotations embodied in critical articles and reviews. For information, address HarperCollins Publishers, 195 Broadway, New York, NY 10007.

HarperCollins books may be purchased for educational, business, or sales promotional use. For information, please email the Special Markets Department at SPsales@harpercollins.com.

Harper Voyager and design are trademarks of HarperCollins Publishers LLC.

FIRST EDITION

Designed by Paula Russell Szafranski

Ward artwork designed by Lauren K. Cannon,
copyright © Peter V. Brett

Library of Congress Cataloging-in-Publication Data has been applied for.

ISBN 978-0-06-274056-4

18 19 20 21 22   LSC   10 9 8 7 6 5 4 3 2 1

For John Brett Jr.

1970–97

It gets easier, but it never gets easy.

Contents

&

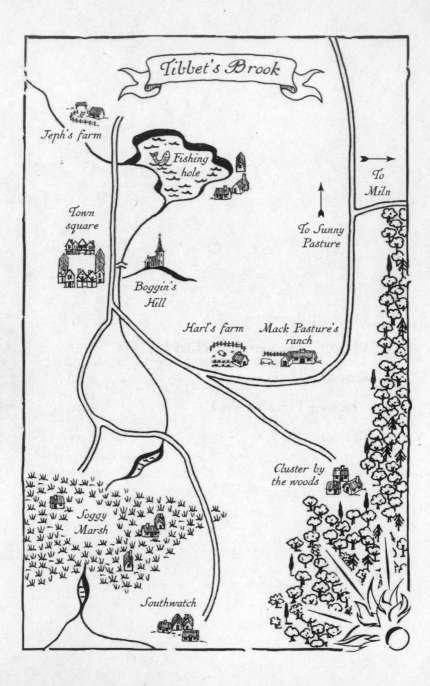

1

Greatward

334 AR SUMMER

Selia shifted, wrapping her arms tighter around the body next to her. Smooth skin with hard muscle beneath, warm like a crock filled with fresh-baked cookies. She put her nose into the thick braid of hair and inhaled. The scent was euphoric.

Selia's eyes popped open.

"Night, girl!" She gave Lesa a shove to wake her. "Fell asleep again!"

Selia glanced at the window, where a faint glow shone through the shutter slats of her house. "Nearly sunup! You've got to get—"

"Shhhhhh." Lesa reached a hand behind her, stroking Selia's face until her callused fingers settled gently on Selia's lips. "Mam and Da went up to Jeph Bales' farm to help prepare. Never know I ent been home."

Lesa snuggled back into the feathered pillow, quickly falling back to sleep. Selia drew a deep breath and curled around her, attempting the same. Lesa was right.

But Selia had never been good at sleeping when there

were problems to worry at. Lesa's parents might be away, but she was still living under their roof. The young woman had barely twenty summers, while Selia was laying stores against her sixty-ninth winter. Lying with another woman was already enough to ignite town gossip. Taking a lover less than a third her age might see folk strip her of the Speaker's gavel—if they didn't just put her out in the night and have done.

Even as Selia squeezed her eyes shut, the sight of Renna Tanner, staked in Town Square for the demons, remained.

No. We don't do that anymore.

But Selia remembered how quickly Jeorje had turned the town against Renna, and he had far more reason to want Selia staked than some barley-headed farm girl.

Selia's arm, tucked beneath Lesa, grew numb. The woman's heat had them both sweating, a sticky bond to their skin. Too uncomfortable to sleep, Selia began the slow process of working her arm free without waking her partner.

Already, she was planning the day. Lesa's family wasn't the only one to head up to Jeph Bales' farm. It was new moon, and Jeph had called the town council to meet on his property that night.

It was an unusual request for the council to meet outside Town Square—not to mention at night. But there were rumors about what Jeph was building on his farm, and all wanted to know the truth of it.

Selia didn't need to guess. Arlen Bales paid his father a visit last moon. She knew this because that same night, Renna Tanner had materialized in Selia's yard, catching her and Lesa with their skirts up.

The Brook's prodigal children brought grave warnings. Smart demons. Shape changers. Corelings working in concert, dismantling wards like Baleses reaping a field. Tibbet's Brook was still coming to grips with fighting even "normal" demons. The battle wards were spreading, but few had tested themselves against the night. Folk weren't prepared for what was coming.

Selia slipped from the bed, quietly padding to the washbasin. Lesa's scent clung to her, evidence of their indiscretion. Renna had stayed hidden until Selia sent Lesa away, and offered no judgment over the tea and cookies, but it was a reminder of how careless they had become.

Folk used to call you Barren, Renna told her, *but tonight's got me wonderin' they got it wrong.*

If Selia and Lesa didn't stop, it was only a matter of time before the town found out. She feared the graybeards might already be recalling old rumors and making guesses.

Selia splashed her face. The water was cold, shocking away the last vestiges of sleep. She looked at her reflection in the same silvered mirror she'd used for almost seventy years, but the face staring back was only dimly familiar—a faded memory brought back to life.

The deep lines in her face had shallowed to nothing. Her once-white hair was yellow at the roots and growing. That hair was a rarity in the Brook, a gift from her father Edwar, a Milnese Messenger who decided to make Tibbet's Brook his home.

Selia looked at her hands. The once-translucent skin was now thick and tough, spots of age melting away into sun-browned flesh.

She straightened, but there wasn't so much as a twinge as her back aligned. No ache in her shoulders and knees. No sparks of pain as her knuckles flexed.

Next to the basin, within easy reach, was the spear

Arlen Bales had given her. She brushed her fingertips over the delicate wards carved into its length, shivering in remembrance of the rush of magic that traveled up its shaft when she struck her first demon with it. The power was wild—intoxicating. In its grip she moved with strength and speed that were . . . inhuman, fighting with animal passion.

The feeling of invincibility faded soon afterward, but a bit of the strength lingered. She woke the next day feeling stronger than she had in years.

Selia had killed many demons since, leading the Town Square militia to victory after victory. Corelings were slowly being cleansed from every yard and field in the Brook.

The rush of magic was addictive, as many folk were learning. Even Selia was caught in its grip. It did more than strengthen the body; it heightened passion as well.

She drew her hand back from the weapon as if it had suddenly grown hot, and looked back at Lesa, snoring contentedly.

Any fool who'd seen a Jongleur's show knew magic came with a price.

"Out of bed, lazy girl." Selia gave Lesa a shove. "Tea is hot and there will be the Core to pay if you let it get cold."

Lesa flung back the covers, shameless as she slipped out of bed and bent to pick up her trousers. She glanced up, smiling as she caught Selia staring.

Selia snatched the blouse from her bedpost and threw it at the girl, but she was smiling, too. "Get dressed while I take the butter cookies from the oven."

Lesa entered the kitchen soon after. Even with her back

turned, Selia could tell the young woman was reaching for the batter-covered spoon resting in the mixing bowl. Without looking up, Selia snatched the spoon and used it to swat the back of Lesa's hand.

"Ow!" Lesa snatched her hand away.

"Licking the spoon's a reward, not a privilege." Selia laid a plate of cookies on the windowsill to cool. "Set the table and pour the tea. Yesterday's batch is in the crock."

Lesa held up a fist, turning it to show the batter splashed across the back. Then she deliberately licked it clean.

Selia raised the spoon threateningly, and Lesa laughed, darting to the cookie crock on the table. "Forget sometimes, you're still Old Lady Barren."

Selia raised a brow. "That what children call me now?"

Lesa colored. "Din't mean . . ."

Selia waved the apology away. "What will your young friends say, when they learn you've been sleeping in Old Lady Barren's bed?"

Lesa winked. "Ent done much sleeping."

"Know what I mean," Selia said.

"You say 'when' like it's written somewhere folk are gonna find out," Lesa said.

"Live to be an old lady, you'll learn folk find everything out eventually."

Lesa threw up her hands. "So what if they do? You're Speaker for the Brook, and every night you go out and kill corelings to keep folk safe. Town couldn't do without you. And I done everything my parents ever asked, and got demon scars to show what I've given this town. Who cares, folk find out we're square girls?"

Selia winced at the term. "Where did you hear that? Do you even know what it means?"

Lesa shrugged. "Everyone knows. Means girls who kiss girls."

Selia bit her tongue. "Schoolyard talk's changed since I was teaching."

Lesa blinked. "You were schoolmam?"

"No." Selia shook her head. "That was Lory, my mother."

Lesa splashed tea as she dunked a cookie, cramming it into her mouth before it had time to soften. Crumbs sprayed as she spoke. "Want to hear all about her."

Selia swatted the air with the wooden spoon. "Ent story time. Sun's coming up. Finish your tea and head out the back before someone sees you. Take Dyer's Way."

Lesa wrinkled her nose. The alley behind Dyer's shop where Jan kept his chemical vats stank, discouraging casual traffic. The perfect path for one wishing to be unseen.

"Don't want to go," Lesa said. "Just tell folk I came at dawn to escort you."

"Since when do I need an escort to walk down the street to Town Square?" Selia gave Lesa *the look*. Her wrinkles might have smoothed away, but her gray hair still carried weight in the Brook.

"Ay, Speaker." Lesa wiped her mouth and left without another word.

You'll pay for that later. Selia let out a breath of relief when the door closed behind the girl. Another moment successfully stolen. How many more would they have?

Her appetite lost, Selia set the cookies aside and took out her writing kit, continuing a series of letters to kin in Fort Miln. There hadn't been a Messenger for over a year, but sooner or later one would come, and her father taught her better than to be unprepared.

After an hour she packed the fresh cookies and went to the stable where Butter, her spirited gelding, waited. Her

father's old Messenger armor was stowed in the saddle-
bags she slung from Butter's back. The Smiths removed
some plates and shifted others, hammering until it all fit
her, but the smell of oil, steel, and old sweaty leather still
reminded Selia of Edwar. There was comfort knowing the
same metal that succored her father on his journeys now
protected her.

His shield was goldwood covered in a layer of fine
Milnese steel, defensive wards still strong after decades of
use and fifty years above the mantel. Only his spear hung
there now, the fine weapon no match for the one Arlen
Bales gifted her.

Selia led her horse down the road to Town Square.
She was thankful for her discretion when she saw Tender
Harral, Meada Boggin, and Coline Trigg already waiting
in the square with the militias. It would not have done for
so many to see her arrive with Lesa.

Meada's son Lucik was with them, along with his wife
Beni, and nearly a dozen men and women from Boggin's
Hill. Their round shields had two concentric rings of
wards, with a frothing mug of ale painted at their center.
The Boggins wore boiled armor with wards burned into
the leather, and kept their warded spears close to hand.

The change magic wrought on Selia was more pro-
nounced, but any fool could see the power at work here,
too. Folk she'd known their whole lives were changing in
noticeable ways. Tender Harral's armor was hung from
an acolyte's horse, but he kept spear and Canon close.
Muscles strained the sleeves of his once-loose robe.

Meada's gray hair was streaked with brown. She led
the Boggin militia in clearing the demons from Boggin's
Hill, but had since given her spear to her son. Lucik was
always a strapping boy, but he'd added fifty pounds of

muscle in recent months. A quiet lad, he was fierce when fighting corelings.

"Speaker." Lucik dropped his eyes when he noticed Selia's gaze. Fierce in battle, yes, but still loyal as a pup.

"Good boy." She resisted the urge to scratch him behind the ears.

Meada snorted as Lucik's ears colored. "Good to see you, Speaker."

"And you, Meada. Sorry I ent been up the hill recently." As she spoke, Selia's eyes scanned the assembled Square militia, mounted five wide and five deep. Twenty-five of her best fighters to keep the peace and stand guard when the sun set. The wards on their wooden shields were a perfect square, a map of Tibbet's Brook painted in the center of its succor.

"Don't think on it," Meada said. "Creator knows you've been busy clearing corelings out of town, and it's got everyone feeling sunnier."

"Credit for that goes to a lot of folk, you and your son included." Selia spotted Lesa in her assigned place in the second row of the formation—close enough to see, but far enough to mask any hint of favoritism. Normally Lesa would meet her eyes and give Selia a private smile, but today the girl had her eyes studiously forward.

She was still upset.

Perhaps that's best, while the council meets.

"Brine sent word not to wait on the Cutters," Harral said. "They'll come in their own time. Hog left at dawn with a dozen store security."

Selia harrumphed. "Store security," Hog called them, but they were fast becoming his personal army. The Square militia was all volunteers, men and women with normal day lives, coming out to fight for their town when the sun set. Most made and warded their own weapons and equipment, with varying degrees of quality.

Hog's store security all wore armor of thick leather, studded with warded silver. Their matching spears were of the finest quality, etched expertly with wards. The three concentric ward circles on their steel-covered shields had in their center a painting of the original General Store Hog built when he first came to Tibbet's Brook.

Store security pulled their weight in town, keeping the square clear of demons and aiding the militia in culling corelings from valuable land, but there was no illusion about whom they answered to.

"Let's not waste time, then." Selia mounted and they set off north.

Jeph's farm was already bustling when they arrived. Hog's pavilion was set, his thick-armed daughters, Dasy and Catrin, selling food and ale. Security was still un loading carts, and Hog himself carried a keg in each arm.

"Night," Coline said. "He looks thirty again."

Hog had always been robust, but he carried more than sixty winters, and in recent years it had begun to show. But, as with Selia, the seasons had melted away with the lines on his face. His hair and beard were coal-black, any last vestiges of gray trimmed away. Thick curls grew on his crown where not long ago there had been bare skin.

"It's unnatural," Coline said. Harral grunted in agreement. Even Meada was nodding.

Selia turned to them, raising an eyebrow.

"That's different and you know it, Speaker," Coline said. "You're out every night, riskin' your life to keep folk safe. Ent the same as payin' store security to drag you a chained-up demon every Fifthday to suck on like a skeeter."

"Ay, maybe," Selia said. "But Hog's always pulled his weight with this town. I'd have run him out for a cheat long ago if he hadn't."

"Ay," Meada agreed. "But don't forget he voted Renna Tanner into the night because he thought it was better for business."

Coline dropped her eyes, losing bluster. For, of course, she had voted Renna out, too. No one, not even Selia, had entirely forgiven her for it.

"Creator plans our trials as well as our triumphs," Harral cut in. "Could be He put Hog here to cast that vote. Might be that's what brought the Deliverer to heal our divisions."

"If that Messenger was the Deliverer I'll eat my cookie crock," Selia said. "Didn't heal a corespawned thing. Brook's more divided than ever."

"That, too, is the Creator's plan," Harral said. "Brook's been evening a long while. Might be it needed to get dark before the dawn."

Selia wrinkled her nose. "*Can't know the Creator's plan,* my da used to say, *but we do know He's not going to come down from Heaven to carry the mail.*"

"What's that supposed to mean?" Coline asked.

"Means we own our problems." Selia locked eyes with the Herb Gatherer. "And our choices."

Coline flinched and dropped her eyes. "Ay, Speaker."

Jeph Bales was showing off his new greatward like a prize pig at the summer Solstice festival. Bales' property was one massive ward of protection now, formed by fences, shrubs, hedges, stone paths, and curve-roofed storage sheds, not to mention the barley fields, manicured from the straight rows of their original planting. Simple shapes flowed seamlessly into one another, creating something altogether more complex. Folk walked around eyes agog as they waited for a turn to climb the watchtower to see the greatward from above.

Jeph broke away from a group of guests when he noticed Selia arrive. "Speaker."

"You're a Speaker now, too, Jeph Bales," Selia reminded him. "You can call me Selia."

Jeph shook his head. "Ent ready for that. Not looking to lead this town."

"Ready or not, Jeph Bales, that's what you're doing. There's more to leading than fancy words. Folk need an example, and you've impressed everyone with this monstrosity you've built."

"Wait till sunset," Jeph said.

There was a shout, and they saw Mack Pasture storming away from Hog, who had his arms crossed. Behind him, two store security guards loomed.

Mack headed their way and Selia sighed. Pasture had become a thorn in everyone's side since he was voted off the council as Speaker for the farms in favor of Jeph.

"Everything all right, Pasture?" Selia called.

"No, it corespawned ent!" Mack cried. "Hog won't sell me a warded spear on credit."

"Could have had your own," Jeph said, "you'd had the stones to stand when the Messenger came." There was no divide in town deeper than those who wanted to protect Renna Tanner and those who voted her into the night.

"Din't need it," Mack snapped, "till Hog bought the old Tanner farm and sent store security to sweep the property. Sent all the corelings runnin' my way, scarin' the cattle and apt to overload the wards. And now he won't so much as rent me a spear."

Selia pursed her lips. She had little more sympathy for

Mack than Jeph, but her father's advice sounded in her head.

Town Speaker speaks for everyone, not just the folk they like.

"I'll have the militia out tomorrow night to start clearing your property," Selia promised.

Next to arrive was Brine Broadshoulders with his adopted son Manie Cutter. Selia remembered the boy, shivering at her table the night corelings breached the wards of the Cluster by the Woods in 319 AR. Manie was a man grown now, tall and heavily muscled, with a warded axe mattock strapped to his back. He and his father led a score of giant Cutters onto Jeph's property.

It was afternoon before the Fishers made their way up the road. Raddock Lawry, their Speaker, was older than Selia, his thick beard stark white, face deep with crags.

Raddock's eyes widened when he saw Selia. She'd shed decades since he saw her last, now looking much as she had when Raddock tried to court her, fifty years ago. "Guess it shouldn't surprise me you've exploited the unnatural, too, Selia."

Selia felt a flash of anger. "I've done nothing but stand up for this town, when you and yours were too stubborn."

So much for speaking for everyone. Anger came easily where Raddock was concerned.

"Punishing Fishers is how you stand up for the town, Speaker?" Garric Fisher was not so old, taller than Selia and half again her weight. He leaned in, trying to intimidate, but Selia hadn't scared easily when she was old and her bones ached. She sure as the Core didn't now.

"Ent punishing anyone." Selia's eyes flicked over his stance, deciding how best to put him on the ground without breaking anything. "Been sending militia to keep Fishing Hole safe, like we agreed."

"Ay, for the Duke's tithe worth of fish!" Raddock growled. "While your militia bullies and robs us."

Selia blinked. "Come again?"

"Drunk on demon magic and looking down on regular folk," Raddock said. "Garric's got Boggins pissing on his fence and leaving demonshit on his doorstep. Other night, someone staked a coreling in my yard. Turned into a rippin' bonfire when the sun came up."

None of this was surprising. The Fishers had turned Tibbet's Brook on its head last year, and a lot of folk resented them for it. Raddock wasn't wrong about what magic did to folk, whetting emotions already sharp.

She blew a breath through her nostrils. "Thank you for bringing it to my attention, Raddock. I'll put a stop to that nonsense straightaway."

"Stopping it ent enough, Selia," Raddock said. "Want to see some punishment. Stam Tailor had Maddy Fisher belowdecks in her father's boat!"

Selia clenched a fist, imagining she was squeezing Stam's throat. "Girl wasn't willing?"

"Don't matter!" Raddock snapped. "She's thirty summers his junior! It's an abomination."

Selia's eyes flicked to Lesa, and this time the girl met the look proudly. She stood with the rest of the Square militia, all of them ready to pounce if the Fishers got out of hand. Raddock caught the glance, taking in the militia with a scowl. The Fishers brought a dozen men with them, but both sides knew they were no match for warriors who killed demons each night.

"Maddy's got nineteen summers, Raddock," Selia said. "Ent for you to say who she should be kissing."

"What about her da?" Raddock demanded. "Tried to break it up and Stam blacked his eye."

Selia pursed her lips. "I'll have a talk with Stam and

get to the bottom of it. If it's like you say, he'll make it right."

"Needs more than talk, Selia," Raddock said. "Law calls for a whippin' in the square.")

Selia shook her head. "Last time we tied someone up in the square, whole town turned upside down. We're better than that."

"Always an excuse why Fishers don't get justice," Raddock sneered. "Ent even botherin' to pretend the town council means spit anymore."

"No one's saying that," Selia said. "But we don't take every dispute to the council, Raddock. Might be this can settle if Stam apologizes, does right by Maddy, and makes some fresh sails for Fishing Hole."

"Don't want rippin' sails," Raddock growled.

"Of course not," Selia said. "All you ever want is blood, Raddock. Ent changed in fifty years."

Raddock's face tightened, wrinkles becoming fissures on the craggy landscape. "Don't want blood, Selia. All I ever want is respect, but that's always been too much to ask."

Not for the first time, Selia's hand itched to punch him in the mouth. After all he'd done when they were young. How *dare* he?

"Fisher's got a point, Selia."

Selia turned to see Jeorje Watch had arrived with fifty armed Watchmen. They wore their traditional garb— bleached white shirts under suspendered black pants, tall black boots, black jackets, and wide-brimmed hats. The jackets were bulkier than a year ago, sewn with plates of warded glass to absorb coreling blows. Their hats were likewise armored, secured by heavy straps.

Coran Marsh was at Jeorje's side, pushed in his

wheeled chair by his eldest son, Keven. Big as Lucik Boggin, Keven had been killing demons since the night the
Messenger gave his father a spear, but though his body
had failed, Coran's mind remained sharp, and it was to
him the Marshes answered.

It was more than a moon since Southwatch annexed
Soggy Marsh, but it was still disturbing to see Marshes
and Watches standing together. Combined, those boroughs counted nearly four hundred of the thousand or so
folk who called the Brook home. A dozen Marsh militia
marched with the Watches, carrying thin, warded fishing
spears.

But it was Jeorje who led them. The oldest person in
the Brook by two decades, Jeorje looked not a day over
thirty. His thin wisps of white hair had been replaced
with a thick mat of nut-brown, his leathern skin smooth
once more. His coat was off, the sleeves of his bleached
white shirt rolled over meaty forearms. Thick muscled bi-
ceps and chest looked ready to split the seams.

He wore no armor, not even a hat, and carried no
shield. The cane he used to stomp to make a point was
like a scepter now, covered in intricate warding, with a
sheathed spear tip at the narrow end. Selia had watched
Jeorje beat corelings to death with that cane.

Selia fixed him with *the look*, though it never affected
Jeorje the way it did others. "Ent one to talk, Jeorje. Hear
tell you just married Mena Watch last month. Girl ent
seen twenty summers."

"*Married*, Selia," Jeorje said. "I don't dishonor wom-
en's families by luring them into fornication."

"Just into your harem," Selia quipped. "Mena is
your . . . sixth?"

"Seventh." There was pride in Jeorje's voice. "A holy

number. And my wife Trena arranged the match with Mena's family personally. I didn't lure her in secret and steal her virtue."

"Only bought it from her da," Selia muttered.

Jeorje ignored the words. "Stam Tailor has ever been a burden on this town, given to drink and poor choices."

Jeorje might be a hypocrite, but he was not without a point. Plenty of folk liked getting drunk on festival days or at night after the wards were checked, but Stam was seldom sober, and someone was always cleaning his mess, one way or the other. He'd taken the rush of magic over drink, but addiction was addiction.

A burden on this town. It wasn't the first time Selia heard Jeorje use those words, and it always led to the same place.

"Fine," she said. "Council's all here now. Send someone to fetch Maddy and I'll send for Stam. We'll hear their case and vote tonight."

It was an empty promise. Hog and Coline were still paying for their votes against Renna Tanner, and Mack had been replaced by Jeph. With those votes turned, the council would never support the Fishers' calls for blood again.

Selia saw a fleeting smile twitch Jeorje's lips, and she realized he had never wanted the vote. He wanted to be seen supporting the Fishers when she was against.

"You need not depend on Town Square for protection from corespawn," Jeorje told Raddock. "Southwatch can offer better."

Selia flexed her knuckles. Adding Fishing Hole would only give Jeorje three council votes out of ten, but half the Brook's population would answer to him. If that happened, the council really would become obsolete, and Selia would be lucky to avoid being staked in the square herself.

"Talk about it on your own time," Jeph cut in loudly. "I called this meeting, and the sun's settin'."

It was crowded atop the watchtower with all ten Speakers and Keven Marsh—who had carried his father up the ladder. Private squabbles died away as they took in Jeph's greatward, clearly visible from above. The symbol brightened as shadows lengthened. By sunset the ward was glowing softly, illuminating all Jeph's property.

Jeph pointed. "Led a couple Wanderers that way last night."

Demons came in all shapes and sizes, but folk in the Brook lumped them into two groups: Regulars and Wanderers. Regulars tended to haunt the same paths, imprinting on an area and almost never leaving. Wanderers hunted where sound and spoor led, ranging wide and without pattern.

Corelings always rose in the same spot they used to flee the sun the night before. As the dark strengthened, black mist vented from the ground like smoke, coalescing into a pair of field demons.

The demons caught sight of people wandering Jeph's yard and tamped their paws to pounce. Folk screamed and fell back, warriors moving forward to put a wall of shields between the demons and the townsfolk.

But as the demons leapt, they were thrown back as the greatward flashed like a bolt of lightning, turning night into day for the barest instant.

Jeph put two fingers in his mouth and gave a shrill whistle. Jeph Young, his eldest son, appeared with a bow, expertly putting a warded shaft into one of the demons. It yelped and collapsed. Its fellow shrieked and clawed at the forbidding, leaving streaks of magic in the air where the claws scraped against the greatward.

The other Bales children appeared with slingshots, peppering the second coreling with warded stones that sparked and bit against its armor. The demon hunched down and attempted to flee, but Jeph Young had another arrow nocked by then, taking it in the back. The downed demon kept kicking until Jeph Young put it down for good with his third shot.

Everyone was impressed by the spectacle. Folk down in the yard gave a cheer, and there was chatter in the watch-tower among the Speakers. Only Jeorje was silent, eyes glittering. No doubt he had come more for politicking than magic, but there was power in Jeph's greatward, and Selia knew the leader of Southwatch would covet it.

And why shouldn't he? The greatwards could make their town's succor a permanent thing. Folk could sleep sound in the night, and tend fields without fear of demons burning them just before harvest. Yet something in that covetous look left Selia unsettled.

When all had ample time for a look, Jeph led them back down to the yard and up onto his porch to address the folk. All eyes were on him, something Jeph Bales had never cared for, but he met those eyes boldly to-night, filled with a sense of purpose Selia had never seen before.

"Messenger taught me a bit of warding before he left last year." No one needed to ask whom Jeph meant. There was only one Messenger who came bearing wards. "Been experimentin' and you can see the results for yourself. Ent no test for these wards. Nothin' to prove. Any as want them can have them. Messenger said they were to be spread far and wide. Said, 'gainst the corelings, we're all on the same side."

There was excited chatter in the crowd at that, but also doubt. Jeph's greatward was ambitious. Many would not feel up to constructing their own when regular wards had done well enough for them thus far.

"That ent all." Jeph's words drowned in the buzz of the crowd.

"Silence." Jeorje didn't shout, but the soft-spoken word was loud, penetrating the din. He thumped his cane on the porch boards for emphasis, and folk froze like cats caught on the kitchen counter.

Jeph didn't miss a beat, raising his own voice. "Messenger told me about corelings we ent seen yet—ones that only come out when the night is darkest. Shape changers that can look like friends and trick folk into stepping beyond the wards. Smart demons that can steal thoughts right outta your head and lead lesser corelings like hounds. Said we need to step up our forbiddings, and gave us the wards to do it. Everyone needs to learn 'em, from the schoolhouse slate to the last elder."

Hog, prewarned, stepped forward. "For those that don't want to wait on lessons, or ent got a steady warding hand, we've got mind wards as stamps, pendants, hat brims, even plates you can glue on your favorite helmet."

"How much you gonna charge for a set o' them plates, Hog?" Mack Pasture shouted.

Hog crossed his arms. "Twenty credits."

The crowd gasped. Twenty credits could feed a family of five for a month. The Brook was prospering as never before, but few in town had that much to spare.

"Always a cheat!" Mack screamed. "Even when Messenger says we're all on the same side!"

There were nods through the crowd, even some of Selia's own militia. Hog's greed was ever getting the better of him.

Selia thumped her spear on the porch, much as Jeorje had. "Ten."

The word bit through the anger in the crowd, all eyes turning toward her. She kept her chin high as Hog scowled, daring him to contradict her.

Rusco Hog was no fool. This wasn't the first time he'd faced an angry crowd, and without Selia to put out the fire he'd have been strung up as a thief long since. He swallowed his grimace and gave a sharp, shallow nod.

"Ten." Jeorje thumped his cane, and Selia, too, had to swallow a grimace. Anytime he could not get the first word, Jeorje was sure to get the last, making every ruling of the town council appear to be his own personal judgment.

He met her look much as she'd met Hog's, calmly daring her to contradict him in front of a crowd.

There was nothing Selia could say without sounding petulant and weak, and Jeorje knew it. Folk outside Southwatch might not like the Speaker, but they were all afraid of him. Old Man Watch held folk to an impossible standard and was quick to punish when they fell short.

"Council better rule on every price in the General Store," Mack called. "Elsewise he'll mark up everythin' else to make up the loss."

Hog lifted a finger, and store security moved to surround him, glowering at any who stepped close. "Don't want to shop at my store, Mack Pasture, ent forcing you."

"Don't matter!" Jeph's shout signaled the end of his patience. "Don't want to pay Hog, Pasture? Learn to draw the rippin' wards yourself! Just said they were free for all."

"Why did the Messenger give all this to you, Jeph Bales, and not the council?" Raddock Lawry asked loudly. "All this talk of demons that look like folk and read minds sounds like a Jak Scaletongue story."

"Might be Scaletongue ent just an ale story," Jeph said.

"Don't answer the question. Why you, Bales?" Raddock wasn't well liked outside his borough, but his white beard was respected, especially when so few of them remained in the Brook. On hearing the question, the crowd wanted an answer, too.

Jeph straightened, meeting Raddock's eye. "Because the Messenger was Arlen Bales. My son."

Even Raddock Lawry and Mack Pasture had nothing to shout in the stunned silence that followed. The Messenger was a revered figure in the Brook. Half the folk thought he was the Deliverer come again, and the rest were still thinking it over. Only a fool would be first to speak.

Jeorje thumped his cane, eyes hard, but whether it was religious fervor or threatening a rival, Selia could not say.

"All know my wife, Silvy, was cored." Jeph pointed to a spot in the yard. "Right there."

Folk standing on the spot shifted uneasily, edging away as if it were cursed.

"What folk don't know is that I stood right here," he stomped a foot on the porch, "safe behind the wards, and watched it happen."

The crowd gave a collective gasp.

"Din't have battle wards back then. Din't think I could do anythin' but die, I went out into a yard full of demons." Jeph shook his head. "But Arlen din't see it that way. Din't see anythin', 'cept his mam in trouble. Ran into the yard and knocked a flame demon off Silvy with a milk bucket and dragged her behind the wards of the pigpen to wait out the night."

Selia saw Jeph's muscles clench, knuckles whitening as he gripped the porch rail.

"When his mam died two days later, Arlen couldn't find it in his heart to forgive me. Creator my witness, can't blame him for that. Ran off and caught Messenger Ragen on his way back to Miln, made his way in the Free Cities."

"Why'd he come back?" someone shouted.

"Found the battle wards, my boy," Jeph said. "Came back to make sure what happened to his mam never happened again. But that ent all." He turned, meeting the eyes of Raddock Lawry and Garric Fisher. "Arlen and Renna Tanner were promised back in 319 AR, just before Arlen ran off. Both of us saw firsthand how Harl Tanner treated his daughters. Locked his girls in the outhouse at night when they were willful, and put hands on them like they were his wives. That's why I took Ilain back with me."

"Din't stop you takin' her to your bed before Silvy's side was cool," Garric growled. "Reckon she witched you with those big bubbies just like Renna Tanner did my son."

"Remember Arlen brought Renna back to my farm, Fisher," Jeph said. "Sat right here and told me she and Cobie wanted to be together, just like the Tender said. Harl killed Cobie, and Renna killed Harl for it before he could kill her next."

"And if the little skink had minded her da, they'd all be alive," Garric snapped. "This town's had enough scandal from Tanner whores."

Lucik Boggin stiffened, eyes flicking to Beni. He turned back to Garric, eyes alight, but Jeph stayed him with a hand. Never a brave man, Jeph moved purposefully down the porch steps toward Garric, and the crowd fell back, clearing a path between the two men.

"Jeph Bales, you get back on this porch!" Selia snapped.

"You may be Town Speaker, but this is my borough and my property, Selia." Jeph never took his eyes off Garric. "Thank you to keep out of this."

Jeorje thumped his cane. "Men have a right to satisfaction." The words were neutral so that whatever the outcome, Jeorje could support it as his own—or the Creator's—judgment.

Jeph kept a firm stride, but Garric, taller and heavier, stood his ground. "Say that again," Jeph growled when they were nose to nose.

Garric shrank back at the words, but Selia could see him dropping his shoulder and setting his feet.

She tensed, ready to cry out or leap from the porch, but something in Jeph's posture stayed her. Her father used to teach boxing to the children in Town Square, and Jeph seemed to remember his lessons. When Garric swung his roundhouse punch, Jeph caught the blow on his curled left arm and then jabbed, stunning the Fisher while a right cross crumpled his nose.

Garric stumbled back but kept his feet. He might have remained in the fight, but Jeph stayed on the attack, stepping in and adding hooks to Garric's body that folded him over and blasted the wind from his lungs. Garric lunged forward, wrapping his meaty arms around Jeph and attempting to twist him to the ground, but Jeph planted his left foot, stopping them cold, and used Garric's hold against him, keeping the Fisher in place to take Jeph's right knee to the chest.

Jeph shoved Garric back and heel-kicked him into the crowd of Fishers surrounding their fighting space. He kept his fists up, but Garric was either unable or unwilling to rise. Jeorje, no doubt hoping for a very different outcome, gave a slight shake of his head.

Coline Trigg ran from the porch, shoving past him to tend to Garric. His broken nose was bleeding freely and had already begun to swell.

"Core's gotten into you, Jeph Bales?" Coline shrieked. "So ashamed of your cowardice you need to act like a demon?"

"Ent a coreling, but I'm through bein' a coward." Jeph raised a finger at Coline. "And you ent got a right to talk down. Known your gatherin' half as well as you claim, my Silvy would've lived and none of this happened."

"That ent fair," Coline said.

"Ay," Jeph said loudly. "Life ent fair sometimes. Wern't fair to my family, or to Cobie Fisher. Ent been fair to the Tanner girls—but that ends tonight. Any that don't like it can get off my property."

"Sayin' your son's the Deliverer?" Raddock moved to stand over Coline and Garric, keeping the crowd's eyes on his injured kin. "Left Fishing Hole behind on purpose?"

"No one's sayin' anything of the sort," Selia cut in. "Fishers left yourselves behind when you set a girl out to be cored without so much as letting her say her piece. Ent too late to see that and go back to the ways things used to be."

Raddock glared at her. "Ent the first time folk've been divided over a girl gettin' cored, is it, Speaker?"

Selia stiffened at the words.

"Yet here you are, right in the middle of it again." Raddock glanced at Selia's militia. "Wonder whose life you'll ruin this time?"

Selia clenched a fist, and it was all she could do not to wade in and pummel the old man much as Jeph had Garric. Her militia, too young to know what Raddock was talking about, looked at each other in confusion, but

Selia wasn't fooled. Raddock hadn't been looking at all the fighters—just the women.

"Ask your elders!" Raddock shouted as Garric was put on a stretcher and the Fishers took their leave.

Jeorje threw Selia a look that was part disgust and partly a deeper hatred. She readied herself, but he said nothing, brushing past her to lead the Watches and Marshes down the road after the Fishers.

Others lingered on Jeph's property, but they kept their distance as the remaining Speakers gathered.

Meada laid a hand on Selia's arm. "Wern't your fault, Selia, no matter what Lawry says."

"What'd he mean, *Ask your elders*?" Jeph said.

Selia sighed. "You ent the only coward with a secret, Jeph Bales. They ever talk about the Square Girls' Club in the schoolyard when you were a boy?"

Jeph blushed. "Ay, but what's that got to—"

"I was the one started it."

2

The Square Girls' Club

284 AR

The sun had chased the demons away, but it was still dark in the shadows under the picnic awning behind the schoolhouse. Selia pressed Deardra Fisher against the wall, kissing her hungrily.

Deardra, more than willing, gripped Selia's hair, threatening to pull the pins free. Selia's heart beat like the feet of schoolchildren at afternoon bell. These stolen moments were what she lived for. Her hand slid down Deardra's back, gripping her bottom through her skirts and pulling her even closer.

"We—" Deardra gasped between kisses. "We need to calm down. Bell's going to ring any moment, and Raddock will come looking if we're not there."

"Let him look," Selia said.

Deardra put her hands on Selia's breasts. Selia tried to lean in, but Deardra pushed her back instead. "Fine sight that would be, his sister out behind the school kissing his promised."

Selia crossed her arms. "Raddock and I ent promised."

"Good as," Deardra said. "Da's going to ask Edwar any day now."

Selia felt a talon in her gut, like a demon trying to claw its way free. "Don't want to marry Raddock."

"Creator, why not?" Deardra asked. "He's sure to be Speaker for Fishing Hole when Da retires. Ent a man in the Brook with better prospects."

"Got prospects of my own." Selia smiled, leaning back in for another kiss. "Don't need a man. Got Deardra Fisher."

Deardra pulled away. "Night, Selia. Square Girls' Club is fun, but it's just till we find husbands. Ent got but two members anyway."

Selia gave a tight smile, trying to hide how the words stung.

Deardra reached out, stroking Selia's arm. "Din't mean—"

Her words broke off as both girls started from the sound of the great bell atop the schoolhouse.

There was a sound of scrabbling feet on the gravel of the yard—young Harl Tanner running barefoot past them and into the school.

Deardra's eyes went wide. "You don't think . . ."

"What's it matter?" Selia pulled free of Deardra's grasp and smoothed her dress. "Just fun till we find husbands, ay?"

"Creator, Selia," Deardra snapped. "You know what—"

"Harl Tanner ent been on time for school a day in his life." Selia turned to head for the door. "Ent no way he got here early enough to peep on us."

Raddock was waiting at the steps when they turned the corner. "Where have you two been? Schoolmam's waiting." A cacophony of children filled the great classroom.

"Just checking the wards." Selia could not keep a snip from her tone at his assumption it was any of his business what she did with her time. He was only a few summers older than her, and they weren't promised, whatever the Fishers might think.

Selia's mother Lory was waiting by the front desk with fifteen-year-old Meada Boggin and a young woman so beautiful Selia's breath caught. Deardra glanced at her, noticing the look with a frown. In a town as small as Tibbet's Brook it was rare to meet someone for the first time, but the woman was in the conservative black skirts and high-necked white blouse and bonnet of Southwatch. They had their own school and Holy House in Southwatch, and some folk went their whole lives without visiting Town Square apart from Solstice festivals.

"About time," Lory said. "Full house today. Asked Meada to throw in with the younger students."

It was Sixthday—market day—and harvest season. The schoolhouse was packed this time of year while parents went to the square to shop. For many children in Tibbet's Brook, market day was their only schooling each week, and Selia's mother worked hard to make it count. Most children learned warding at home, but few had letters, or maths past counting livestock.

"This is Anjy Watch." Lory gestured to the young woman. "She'll be staying in the room upstairs for a few seasons, helping teach the Watches who come for market day. Selia, will you show her—"

"Of course," Selia blurted.

"Wonder what's wrong with her," Deardra snipped, "watches want to be rid of her for a few seasons?"

"Looking for a husband," Raddock guessed. "Watches send the pretty ones sometimes, when they want to hook strong young backs to add to their numbers."

"Ent *that* pretty," Deardra muttered.

Lory rapped her straightstick on the desk, and the din of children quieted. "Everyone fetch your slates."

There was chaos as dozens of dirty children, many of them barefoot, bustled around the slate piles and fetched chalk from the dusty bin, streaking dirty coveralls and skirts with the white powder.

The students in from Southwatch were the exception. Their white shirts and blouses were clean and bright, boots and shoes polished to shine. There were no patches or holes in their charcoal-gray pants and skirts. Each had their own slate, chalk held ready without a sign of it on their clothes.

The Watches sat quietly in neat rows, eyes on the schoolmam, and Lory rose to the occasion, teaching advanced reading and mathematics to the older students while Selia and the other teaching assistants broke the rest into groups for more remedial lessons.

Anjy took the younger Watch children. Selia watched a bit longer than was proper, pulling her eyes away and turning back to her group hoping no one noticed. "You have one hundred and fifty cattle."

"Ent got half that many," Mack Pasture said.

"Figuratively," Selia explained patiently. "Imagine you have one hundred and fifty cattle."

Mack closed his eyes, brow knotting as he struggled to envision such wealth. He began to smile. "All right."

Selia fought the urge to roll her eyes. "You sell ten percent of them. How many do you have left?"

The smile left Mack's face. He opened one eye, as if reluctant to let his imagined cattle go. "One hundred . . . forty?"

"One thirty-five, idjit." Harl Tanner spat.

"That's enough out of you, Harl Tanner!" Selia

snapped. "What did I tell you would happen, you spat on the schoolhouse floor again?"

Harl's face went deathly pale. "Ay, please. Don't tell my da. It'll be the outhouse for sure!"

Selia didn't know the term, but she could guess its meaning well enough. Young Harl was more apt to instill fear than feel it. If he was afraid of his father, there was good reason. "Then that floor had best be scrubbed clean."

Harl was on his knees with a bucket and brush when Lory rang the bell and the other children spilled out into the yard.

Raddock and the other teaching assistants came to stand by Selia as the children filed past. "You should tell his father anyway."

Selia thrust her chin Harl's way. "Why, when the threat of it is enough to pull the wood?"

"Da says lessons don't set in without a trip to the woodshed," Raddock said.

"Tanners call it the outhouse," Selia said.

"Whatever they call it, Tanner needs a whupping." Raddock said the words loud enough for Harl to hear, and the boy looked up.

The brush fell into the bucket with a splash as Harl got to his feet, advancing on Raddock. "What's that, Fisher? Reckon I din't hear it right."

Raddock had twenty-two summers to Harl's thirteen, but he shrank back at the dead stare Tanner leveled his way. It was only when he noticed Selia watching that Raddock steeled himself and took a step forward. "Said your father's going to hear about this."

Harl laughed. "That I spat on the floor? Ent nothin' compared to what he'll do he hears I let a stinkin' Fisher talk down to me."

Raddock stuck a finger in Harl's face. "Listen here, you little—"

He screamed as Harl grabbed the finger and yanked it aside, fist flicking out to crack against the older boy's eye socket. As Raddock stumbled back, Harl bared his teeth and leapt on him, taking them both to the floor.

"Enough!" There was an audible crack as Lory's straightstick whipped across Harl's shoulders. The boy screamed and Selia tensed, ready to interpose herself as he turned that feral gaze toward her mother.

Lory was uncowed. Again the straightstick fell, and Harl hopped off Raddock with a yelp. "Out of my schoolhouse, Harl Tanner, and don't you expect to be let back in until your mother comes to see me!" The stick cracked against his backside. Harl scurried past the exiting students and out the door, laughter at his back.

"Night, I think he broke my finger," Raddock moaned.

"Serves you right," Lory snapped. "Selia had Harl in hand until you saw fit to make yourself the law."

"Ay, mam. Sorry, mam." Raddock cradled his right hand in his left. The index finger did indeed look crooked.

"Let me have a look." Lory took a firm hold of the hand, examining. "Dislocated, not broken. Take it to Sallie Trigg and she'll give you something to bite on while she sets it right."

"I'll drown that little piece of demonshit," Raddock growled as they followed the children out the door.

"Wouldn't bet on it." Deardra nodded to Harl, who had joined the boys and the handful of girls who clustered in the yard for Edwar's weekly boxing lesson. "Harl's learning to break noses while you bury yours in books."

"Your mother kicked him out," Raddock complained. "That should mean boxing, too. Tell the Speaker—"

"If Father needs to be told, Mother will do it," Selia said. "See what happens if you take it on yourself to do it for her."

"It'll be the outhouse." Deardra laughed. Raddock glared at his sister, air hissing through his broad nostrils.

"Grandfather would strip that boy's hide off for fighting in the classroom," Anjy said.

"Grandfather?" Selia asked. Anjy pointed to Jeorje Watch, standing with Selia's father and Tender Stewert while the children assembled for the lesson. Edwar beckoned them over.

"I don't know why you insist on teaching this barbaric sport to children," Tender Stewert was saying. He was slender in his plain brown robes, a city-trained Tender come to the Brook to spread the Creator's word.

"Ent a sport, Tender." Jeorje was tall and stood straight as a post, looking down to meet the Tender's eyes. "Man needs to know how to defend himself. *Creator defends best those who keep a spear at the ready.*" Jeorje was the shady side of sixty, his trim black beard streaked with gray, matching the stark contrast of his black and white suit.

"Defend against who?" Stewert broke eye contact, looking instead to the sky. "*In time of Plague, all men must be as one.*"

"Ay," Jeorje agreed, "by ridding ourselves of the sinners that brought it about." He pointed with his cane at a small group of female students. "It's teachin' girls that ent Canon."

"I teach whoever wants to learn." Edwar nodded at the young woman by Jeorje's side. "Good for a girl to know how to step back and throw a right hook when a boy won't take no for an answer."

Anjy's eyes widened at that. She spread her skirts and dipped. "Please, Grandfather, may I take the lesson?"

"Absolutely not." Jeorje crossed his arms and threw Edwar a sour look. "Girl's hook is the least a Southwatch boy needs to worry about, he's fool enough to lay hands on anyone ent his wife."

"Honest word," Edwar agreed. "Selia, Anjy's never been to market on her own. Why don't you and the others show her around?"

"Of course," Selia said. "We're headed that way now. Raddock . . . jammed his finger, and needs to see the Triggs."

"Your father won't let you box, either?" Anjy asked as they headed up the road to Town Square at Raddock's angry pace.

"I get private lessons," Selia said. "Da doesn't want the boys to know what I can do."

"Boy's in for a surprise, he tries to get his hands on this!" Deardra gave Selia's bottom a squeeze, and they both laughed. Raddock scowled, but Meada was used to it, and kept her eyes on the road ahead. Anjy's face colored, but she did not look away.

Deardra gave Selia a wink. "What brings you to town, Anjy?"

"Grandfather says it's past time I found a husband," Anjy said. "But there ent a lot of boys my age in Southwatch. Says no granddaughter of his is going to be someone's second wife."

"Corespawned right," Deardra said.

Anjy gasped at the blasphemy, but said nothing.

"So you've come looking for love," Selia said.

Anjy shrugged. "Grandfather says love grows out of a good match."

"He's right." Raddock's eyes were on Selia as he said the words.

Selia put her hands on her hips. "And what would you know of it, Raddock Fisher?"

Raddock said nothing, picking up the pace even more. Town Square was packed with carts and booths as hundreds of folk gathered to barter their goods. There was shouting and laughter, the smells of hot food and fresh produce mixed with the stench of animals and the hiss of hot iron quenched. More than a few hagglers seemed close to blows, unable to agree on the relative value of what they had to trade.

Anjy stopped short, and the others kept on a few steps before noticing. "It's so . . . crowded."

"You'll get used to it," Selia promised as she and Deardra took the Watch girl's arms from either side and guided her into the press. Anjy's head swiveled back and forth, taking in the sights as they followed Raddock to the Triggs' booth.

Harve Trigg was a kind man not yet forty, with gentle hands and dirty fingernails. He worked the front of the booth, tending his potted plants and powdered herbs, mixing cures and brewing tonics. He took one look at Raddock's bent finger and sent them in back.

Sallie Trigg, the town midwife, was bigger than her husband, with thick meaty arms. She glared sternly at Raddock when he showed her his finger. "Been fightin'?"

"No, mam," Raddock said.

"Harl Tanner did the fightin', after Raddock mouthed off to him," Deardra gladly supplied, drawing a glare from Raddock.

"Best steer clear of that one," Sallie said. "Boy keeps me busier than I'd like." She gave Raddock a strip of leather. "Bite this."

No sooner had Raddock taken it in his teeth than Sallie gave his finger a firm yank, setting it back in its proper socket. "Grrrmph!"

"All done," Sallie said, wrapping the hand in cloth. "Best go easy on it for the next few days. Should hurt like the Core, but it won't give you lasting trouble."

"Ay, Selia," Bil Square called as they passed his market stall. Bil and his mother made the best quilts in the Brook.

"Let's go." Raddock put a hand on her shoulder.

"Nonsense." Selia shook the hand free, moving over to Bil. He was of an age with the rest of them, shorter than Selia and slighter than Raddock. "What can I do for you, Bil?"

"Hopin' you might speak to your da for me," Bil said. "One of Mam's quilts went missin' off the line. Heard from Mabul Grover she saw it on Nile Digger's bed."

This wasn't the first time someone came to Selia with grievances they were not ready to escalate to her father. Edwar encouraged it. *Speaker training*, he called it. "Leaving aside what Mabul was doing in Nile's bedroom," Selia said, "have you spoken to Nile?"

Bil dropped his eyes. "No."

"Da's a busy man, Bil," Selia said. "Speaker's job is to hold folk to the law, not solve all your problems. Come to me with proof Nile stole your quilt and won't pay its worth, I'll take you to see Edwar. But he ent got patience for folk can't be bothered to try 'n' resolve their own disputes."

Bil nodded. "Ay, Spea—" He checked himself. "Selia. Thank you."

"Think no more on it," Selia said.

"Never liked that little seamstress," Raddock growled as they continued down the path. "I tell you he offered to pull me off behind his stall?"

Deardra laughed. "Ought to let him next time. Maybe then you wouldn't have to do it yourself behind the bait shack."

Raddock turned purple as Selia barked a laugh, and even Anjy hid a smile behind a delicate hand.

Ĕ

The others had drifted off home as the afternoon wore on. Selia walked Anjy back to the school and up to the small apartment by the bellhouse.

"Ent much," Selia gestured to the bed, dresser, and writing desk, "but it's warm and dry." She pulled the curtain from the window. "And you can see all Town Square from up here." She grinned at Anjy's appreciative gasp.

"It's wonderful," Anjy said.

"Seems an odd way to find a husband," Selia said.

"Eh?" Anjy asked.

"Sending you on your own to work with children instead of just asking help to find a match," Selia said. "Mam won't take kindly to you bringing young men up here."

"Won't be a problem," Anjy said. "Grandfather just thought it best I spend a little time away from Southwatch."

"Trouble with a boy?" Selia asked.

Anjy did not meet her eyes. "Ay, something like that."

Selia gave her hand a squeeze. "Don't owe me explanations and I won't press, but I ent one to judge. Be your friend, you'll have me."

Anjy did meet her eyes then, flashing a smile that sent a thrill through Selia. She floated down the steps on it, only to find Harl Tanner in the classroom, banging out the erasers, hands white with chalk.

Selia put her hands on her hips. "Know you're not allowed in here, Harl Tanner."

"Cleaned the blackboard," Harl said. "And swept the floor."

"All well and good." Selia pointedly took a heavy key out of her pocket. "But I'm locking up now."

Harl did not protest, replacing the erasers on their ledge and allowing her to shoo him out the door.

Selia half turned, keeping one eye on the boy as she locked the schoolhouse door. "Shouldn't you be off home? Long walk, and the corelings won't wait."

"Need you to talk to your mam," Harl said.

Selia slipped the key into a deep pocket in her dress. "Only one needs to talk to my mam is yours."

"I'll do anythin'." Harl sounded desperate. "Haul privy buckets. Chop wood. Whatever she needs."

"None of that makes up for attacking a teacher, Harl."

"Don't know what Da's like," Harl said. "Be a week in the outhouse, he finds out."

"That's why Lory asked to speak to your mam instead," Selia said.

"She'll tell him. Knows better'n to keep something like that from him."

Selia crossed her arms. "Should have thought of that before you dislocated Raddock's finger."

Harl's face darkened. "Tell your secret."

"What secret?" Selia snapped.

"That you play kissy with Raddock's sister behind the schoolhouse," Harl said.

Selia felt her stomach clench, but it was followed by a flash of anger. "Don't threaten me, you corespawned little brat!" Selia stepped in, raising a fist, and Harl shrank back. "I'm not Raddock Fisher. I'll put your teeth out, and your da will put you in the outhouse for a month for spreading lies!"

"Ent a lie," Harl said. "Seen it."

"Who will folk believe?" Selia demanded. "Speaker's and schoolmam's daughter, or the little rat who spits on the floor and attacks teachers?" She gave him a shove. "Run on home before you make things even worse for yourself."

Harl's nostrils flared and his eyes slitted. Selia could see he was readying to attack and put her fists up. "Try it."

Instead, Harl spat on the ground, turned, and ran, smacking the wardpost in frustration as he headed up the road.

There was a rustle of cloth, and Selia glanced up to see the curtain of Anjy's room move.

Selia started awake at the ringing of the great school bell. Her room was pitch-dark, but she groped until she found her dress and pulled it on, stumbling out the door even as her father burst into the common. The hearth had burned down to embers, but she caught a glint of metal in the dim glow and knew Edwar was pulling on his armor.

Selia put a taper into the fireplace and lit a lamp, moving quickly to help Lory with the fastenings. "What's happening?"

"Schoolhouse wards are lit up like a Solstice bonfire," Edwar said, "and there's smoke in the air."

"Corelings?" Selia's heart went cold. Anjy was in there, alone.

"Must be." Edwar stuck an arm through his shield and snatched his spear off the mantel.

I locked the door. The thought flickered in Selia's mind, and before she knew it, she was reaching for the spare shield. It was wood, not steel like her father's, but its wards were strong. "I'm going with you."

"Like night you are." Lory stepped in front of the shield, arms crossed. "Let your father handle this." Edwar went to her, and she kissed him hard on the mouth. "Come back to us."

"I love you," Edwar told them both, then turned and faded into the night. Selia and Lory stared after him, catching glimpses of his hunched form in the flashes of wardlight and the evil orange glow coming from up the road.

But then Selia heard Anjy's scream, and staring wasn't enough. Before her mother could stop her, she snatched up the spare shield and ran into the night.

"Selia Square! Get back here!"

Selia ignored her cries, running as her father did, low and quiet. Lights were appearing in windows as folk looked to see what was happening, but none were foolish enough to leave the safety of their wards.

She caught up to her father as he crouched by the broken fence. One of the wardposts was broken, but there was no sign of flame. It had simply been shattered, allowing demons into the schoolyard. Selia counted three—two flamers and a looming rock—but their cries were sure to draw others. Against the moonlit sky, Selia glimpsed a wind demon circling the lamplit bellhouse atop the school where the great bell continued to clang.

If she's ringing the bell, she's alive, Selia thought. *Ent too late.*

"Corespawn it, Selia!" Edwar growled. "I told you to stay inside."

"Anjy's all alone," Selia said.

"And I would better be able to help her without you." Edwar spat, but he didn't argue further.

"What are the demons waiting for?" Selia asked.

"The flamers have set fire to the house, but the wards are holding for now." Edwar lifted his spear. "Keep your shield up and follow close."

The rock demon lunged at the great schoolhouse door, but the wards flared, and it was thrown onto its back. "Now!" They ran for the door, Edwar's shield on his left arm, Selia's on her right. One of the flame demons leapt at Edwar, but it was no more than twenty pounds, and he batted it aside with his shield. The wards flashed, and the coreling was knocked across the yard.

The other flame demon spat fire at Selia, but she had her shield ready, deflecting the firespit as she ran. It bounced off, but a glob of the sticky stuff landed on the hem of her dress, and the cloth blazed.

Selia shrieked, stumbling as they reached the schoolhouse steps. Edwar kept his wits, hauling her up the steps past the wardnet. He stomped on the skirt and swung his spear, the long blade slashing away the burning section. Then he reached a gauntleted hand for the door. "Locked."

"Got the key." Selia fished it from her dress pocket, but when she tried to put it in the lock, the metal was hot and burned her unprotected fingers. She cried out, dropping the key.

"Flame's on this side of the building," Edwar said.

"We can go around back . . ." Selia ventured.

"Not with demons in the yard," Edwar said. "Step away from the door."

He went to the window first, putting the steel-capped

butt of his spear through the panes. Then he put up his
shield and gave the door a heavy kick from his armored
boot. Wood splintered and caved, but the door held. He
took a step back, raising his shield, and smashed through,
crashing to the schoolroom floor.

Selia felt a blast of heat as fire coughed from the doorway. Smoke began to pour from the broken windowpanes.
She soaked her kerchief in the rain barrel, tying it about
her face before she darted in. Inside, fire was spreading
through the classroom, greasy smoke thick in the air. The
heat was nearly unbearable. But no doubt it was worse
for Edwar. His armor might have protected him from the
burning door, but soon the metal would heat and cook
him alive if they did not escape.

"Keep close to the floor!" Edwar shouted, and Selia
hunched low, gulping the cleaner air as they made their
way toward the stairs.

"Anjy!" Edwar boomed. "Anjy Watch!"

There was no reply, the bell continuing to clang as
the girl desperately hauled on the rope in hope of rescue. There was a crash as the rock demon made another
attempt to cross the smoke-weakened wards. The whole
schoolhouse shook and the porch railings snapped. The
coreling howled as magic arced like lightning across
its body, but it pressed on through. Edwar himself had
smashed the next line of defense, and the giant demon
shattered the doorway as it burst into the classroom.

"Go!" Edwar gave Selia a push toward the stairs as he
got to his feet. "I'll lead it out the back!"

It seemed a mad plan, but as the rock swiped at her
father, his shield blazed with magic, turning the blow.
He jammed his spear into its open mouth and the demon howled with pain, biting down and shattering the

weapon. It spun, lashing at him with its heavy tail, but the wards on Edwar's armor lit up. He was knocked aside, but kept his feet, banging his heavy gauntlet against his shield, drawing the demon after him as Selia hurried up the stairs.

But the rock was not the only threat. The flame demons scurried after Selia like dogs chasing a cat, leaving fresh fires in their wake.

The smoke was less thick on the second floor, drawn by the draft from the broken door and window, but Selia knew that would not last as the flames spread. "Anjy!" she screamed.

The ringing slowed as she approached the rope room. Selia pulled on the door, but it was barred from the inside. She pounded her fist against the wood as the demons closed on her.

The door opened as a demon leapt at her. Selia braced behind her shield and shoved hard, knocking it back long enough to fall into the room. Anjy slammed the door shut and dropped the bar, but a pair of talons pushed like nails through the wood, and Selia knew it would not hold.

"We're trapped!" Anjy cried.

"Up the ladder to the belfry!" Selia cried. It might only delay the inevitable, but where there was life there was hope. Anjy recovered her wits and began to climb. Selia slung her shield over a shoulder and followed as the door blackened and another blow cracked the boards.

A final press, and the two flame demons burst into the tiny rope room. Smoke followed in their wake, drawn to the open shaft. The corelings attempted to climb the ladder, but even nimble flamers could not scale the rungs without hands. They clawed the walls instead, scaling the sheer face nearly as fast as the young women could climb.

"What now?" Anjy cried as they made the belfry. Below, the town spread out before them, a light in every window, but no one coming to help.

"Haul up the rope." Selia pulled the shield off her shoulder, watching the demons climb. Even amid the smoke and darkness, their glowing eyes and mouths marked them clearly.

She waited as Anjy pulled the rope, muscles knotting as the glowing eyes grew closer, closer. Selia waited until they were almost upon them. The lead demon hawked fire and closed its eyes to spit, and in that moment she threw her shield. It struck the demon full in the face, flame wards flashing as it knocked the demon from its perch. The demon fell into the other, both of them tumbling back down into the rope room with the precious shield.

The demons were unharmed, rolling immediately to their feet and leaping back onto opposite walls, climbing again.

Selia snatched the rope from Anjy, hurling it over the rail and down to the sloping roof. The bell rang again as she pulled it taut and hopped up to sit on the rail and swing her skirts over. "Follow me."

Anjy looked over the rail doubtfully. The rope was enough to get off the tower to the roof, but it would not see them safely to the ground. She froze.

Selia put out a hand. "Trust me."

Anjy took the hand and Selia hauled her up, leading the way down the rope. A wind demon shrieked from above as their feet skidded against the steeply sloping shingles. There were wind wards cut into each tile to keep a demon from landing on the roof, but they would not stop it from snatching one of them up and winging away.

Selia took a few quick steps, then released the rope, wrapping her arms around Anjy. "Let go!"

Selia could not tell if Anjy complied or if it was her own sudden added weight that cost Anjy her grip, but they fell away even as a wind demon struck the warded shingles where they had just been.

The demon's shrieks matched Selia and Anjy's as all three tumbled down the roof, but Selia had angled them carefully. She and Anjy dropped over the lip and fell just a few feet, landing on the more gently sloping picnic awning under which she and Deardra had shared kisses what seemed a lifetime ago. The breath was knocked from them, but Selia grabbed at the gutter as they rolled from the awning edge. Her arms screamed and her grip could not hold, but she broke their momentum enough for them to hit the ground bruised but unbroken.

Anjy opened her mouth, but Selia slapped a hand over it, hauling them up and putting their backs to the hot schoolhouse wall as she scanned the yard. There was a crash from inside and the whole building shook. The rock demon roared, and she suddenly remembered her father, fear gripping her. Had her foolish insistence on coming along cost Edwar's life?

But then one of the doors to the cellar slammed open, and Edwar climbed out with a groan. Inside, she could hear crashing and roars, but the cellar was cramped, and the demon would need to dig its way out.

Edwar caught sight of them as Selia ushered Anjy his way. "Creator be praised."

❦

Lory shrieked at her when they got back, but she did it with her arms wrapped around them both, tears streaking her face. Then she calmed, lips tight as she examined them, cleaning, stitching, and binding scrapes and cuts.

"You'll sleep with Selia until we get things sorted, Anjy," Lory said when the work was done. "Get some rest. Going to be a long day tomorrow."

They went into Selia's room, and Anjy threw her arms around her the moment they were alone, sobbing. Selia guided them to the bed and sat, holding her until the shuddering eased.

Anjy looked up at her, her big eyes wide and beautiful, wet with tears. "Wasn't trouble with a boy."

"Eh?" Selia asked.

"Why Grandfather sent me from Southwatch," Anjy clarified. "It wasn't a boy." She put her hand on Selia's, soft and gentle. "It was a girl."

She lifted her chin, and then Selia was kissing her, and everything they'd been through was forgotten in the rush of realization.

Anjy was a square girl, too.

❦

"Night," Anjy gasped. "Where'd you learn that?"

Selia moved up to lie by her side. Both were sweating, even in the chill night. "Got a tanned bottom for walking in on Da doing it to Mam. Heard her tell Sallie Trigg it was a trick he learned on his Messenger travels."

"That's . . . some trick. Don't know how I kept quiet at the end," Anjy said. Selia laid her head against the young woman's chest, listening to the rapid beat of her heart. "You do that with Deardra?"

Selia stiffened, but Anjy put a gentle hand on her head, stroking her sweaty hair. "It's all right."

"Heard what Harl said?" Selia asked.

"Ay, but didn't have to," Anjy replied. "Saw how you two look at each other, way you touch. It was like that with Sementhe."

"Girl who got you sent from Southwatch."

Anjy gave a nervous laugh. "Truer is her husband was the problem. Caught us kissing in the bath, and you'd have thought he found corespawn in the tub."

"So you're . . . free," Selia said.

"Ay, free as a square girl can be." Anjy sighed. "Free until Grandfather can settle things down and find a husband to take a shamed woman. Are you?"

"Am I what?" Selia asked.

"Free," Anjy said. "Deardra—"

"—told me being a square girl was just fun until we could find husbands," Selia said. "Wants me to marry her brother."

"Raddock?" Anjy held her nose.

"Ay." Selia smiled. "Core will freeze before I promise that pompous Fisher."

"So you're . . . free." Anjy flashed that smile, and Selia kissed her again.

6

The schoolhouse had burned to the ground by the time morning banished the demons back to the Core. Selia went with her parents to view the wreckage, and Lory wept at the sight.

Edwar laid a hand on her shoulder. "We'll rebuild, love."

There was a crowd of onlookers, but Edwar had men keep them back while he inspected the scene. "Here." He pointed to the shattered wardpost they had seen the night before. "This is where the breach occurred."

Lory squatted to examine the post. "There's chalk on the ward."

Selia felt her stomach clench, remembering Harl Tanner's chalk-covered hands. Had he purposely marred the ward? It was a heavy accusation to lay without evidence—especially since Harl could strike back with accusations of his own.

Isak Fisher, the Speaker for Fishing Hole, arrived soon after with his children, Raddock and Deardra. "Everyone all right, Edwar?"

"Burned and bruised," Edwar said, "but nothing lost that can't be rebuilt."

"And better than before," Isak agreed. "Wood and stone are nothing next to our lives. Which is why I think it's time we spoke."

Edwar looked at Raddock, standing respectfully back, eyes down, as if noticing him for the first time. "Let's go back to the house and put the kettle on. Selia, why don't you take Deardra and Anjy back to your room for a spell?"

Selia's jaw tightened, but she knew better than to cause a scene. "Of course, Father."

"You all right?" Deardra asked, taking Selia's arm to examine the bandaged burn as they walked.

"Lucky to be alive," Selia said. "Two flame demons and a rock breached the schoolhouse wards."

"And you were . . ." Deardra swallowed, ". . . there?"

"Couldn't just leave Anjy to them," Selia said.

"Came in like the Deliverer himself," Anjy said.

Deardra glanced at the young Watch woman as they entered the house and went to Selia's room. She took in the rumpled bedclothes and the torn dresses on the floor. She sniffed the air as if she could smell what they had done over the stink of smoke that clung to the cloth.

"You slept here?" Deardra's eyes bored into Anjy.

"What of it?" Anjy asked, but there was guilt in the sudden flush to her skin.

Deardra balled a fist. "Think you know what."

"Don't see why you care, if you brought your da and Raddock to discuss what I expect." Selia's words pulled Deardra's eyes back to her. "'Sides, said yourself there weren't enough members in the Square Girls' Club."

"Din't mean you should go and bed some starch-necked Watch skink!" Deardra snapped.

"Ay!" Anjy cried.

"Just fun till we find husbands." Selia failed to keep the bitterness from her words. "Ent that what you said? That it don't mean anything?"

"Don't." Deardra spat on the floor. "And you'll be promised soon enough." She gave a nod back to the door.

Selia crossed her arms. "See about that."

"Say no, and I'll see the whole rippin' town knows why," Deardra growled.

"And tell your own part in it?" Selia asked. "That you put horns on your own brother, letting him shine on the girl you were kissing?"

Deardra planted her hands on her hips. "Your word against mine."

"Harl Tanner knows," Selia said.

"Eh?" Deardra looked shaken.

"Caught us behind the schoolhouse yesterday," Selia said. "Threatened to tell, I didn't find a way to get him back in school without his da finding out."

"Night," Deardra breathed, her anger dissipating.

"Tell tales and we'll all be in for it," Selia said.

"Got it all covered, then." There were tears in Deardra's eyes. "Selia Square gets what she wants, and the Fishers can hang."

"Ent like that, Deardra." Selia reached for her, but Deardra batted the hand away, turning and leaving the room. Selia turned to Anjy, but the girl refused to meet her eyes.

❧

"It's a good match," Lory said.

"Ay, maybe," Selia said. "But I don't love him."

"Phagh." Lory fanned the air. "Nineteen summers to your name. Don't know what love is. Love comes from building a home together. From living for someone else. It's a seed, watered by years and shared responsibility."

"Ent how you and Da tell it," Selia said. "Da didn't quit his Messenger job and sell his house in Miln to come plant a seed and wait years to see if it grew."

"Ay, you've the right of that," Edwar agreed.

"Stay out of this," Lory said.

"I won't," Edwar said. "It was my blessing Isak came for, and I gave it thinking it was what Selia wanted. If it ent . . ." He spread his hands.

Selia threw her arms around him. "Thank you, Da."

"You sure about this, sunshine?" Edwar asked. "Fishers are apt to be steamed, I take it back. Ent a thing to do if you're still thinking."

"Had years to think on it," Selia said. "Don't want Raddock."

"Then who do you want?" Lory demanded. "Ent a child anymore, Selia. Time you started a family."

Edwar laid a hand on Lory's shoulder. "Peace, love. One worry at a time."

"Worry about where I'm going to teach, next," Lory said.

"It can wait a few days until we—" Edwar began.

"Can't," Lory cut him off. "Know these folk better'n you, Edwar. Most of 'em think schooling's a waste of time already. Won't send their kids back, they lose the habit."

❧

There was an old barn, unused since Mart Bales had passed on. Before the first day was through, Edwar had an army of folk clearing it out, sweeping the floor, and shoring up the wards. Others built a wooden frame and, once it was hauled from the wreckage, six men lifted the great bell atop it. At dusk, Lory pulled the bell herself, letting folk know school would be back in session the next day.

"Stubborn, your mam," Anjy said that night, as she and Selia shared kisses in the darkness of her room.

"Runs in the family," Selia said.

They stayed up late into the night, talking between kisses, asking questions, falling deeper and deeper as they bared their lives to one another.

"Don't want to marry, that means a man," Selia said. "Be a lonely spinster first."

"Spinster, ay, maybe." Anjy tightened her embrace. "Don't think you'll be lonely."

As Selia drifted off to sleep, she felt a peace such as she had never known.

❧

A crowd of children were gathering at the barn the next morning when Raddock and Deardra appeared, their expressions cold.

"Here to help school back to its feet, mam," Raddock said, "but come next season, you'll need to find new teachers."

"You're a good man, Raddock," Lory said.

For the rest of the day, Raddock refused to meet Selia's eyes, and Deardra glared needles at Anjy. Selia kept as far from Anjy as possible, but every now and then they would catch each other's eye when no one was looking and share a secret smile.

Raddock didn't linger at the afternoon bell. Deardra looked like she might want to stay and have words with Selia, but Raddock practically dragged his sister along with him as he hurried away.

"All right?" Anjy asked. "You look sad."

"Deardra and Raddock are my friends," Selia said. "Never meant to hurt them."

"Ent your fault you don't want Raddock," Anjy said.

Or Deardra didn't want me, Selia thought.

Tensions remained all week, but Raddock and Deardra always left promptly at the bell, and no sooner were they around the bend in the road than Anjy slipped her hand into Selia's. They were inseparable after that, whether it be chores or the long hours by the hearth in the common, after Edwar and Lory retired. They talked quietly but eagerly, breathless in anticipation of heading to bed together.

Market day came around again and Fern Tanner showed up with her son Harl. The boy looked pale and haggard, with dark circles under his eyes. Was that the look of guilt, or one who had spent a week in the Tanner outhouse for spitting and fighting at school? Was it thoughtlessness or malice that led him to mar the wardpost? The former was punishable, but the latter was . . . monstrous. Selia didn't want to believe anyone in the Brook capable of such a thing.

Lory went to greet Mrs. Tanner. "Fern, thank you for coming. Harl, wait out here while I speak with your mother. Selia, take the other children inside and start lessons."

Selia had no choice but to comply, casting a nervous glance at Harl, standing not five feet from Raddock.

Lory and Fern were in the back room for a long time. There were occasional raised voices, too muffled to make out. Fern was red-faced as she left the barn, but a moment later, Harl entered and took a seat with the other children. He looked up at Selia and gave her a dark smile.

Selia turned and saw Raddock enter the barn, face red and twisted. He stormed over to where Deardra was preparing slates and grabbed her hard by the arm. She tried to pull away, but Raddock was larger and stronger, dragging her out the side door to talk privately.

Lory came out of her makeshift office to take over lessons, and Selia hitched up her skirts, hurrying out the side door. Raddock had Deardra against the wall, looming over her. "Let her go, Raddock."

Raddock looked at her, then shoved Deardra so hard she stumbled and would have fallen if Selia hadn't rushed to catch her. There was no gratitude in Deardra's eyes for the save. She shoved Selia just as hard, and the three of them stood glaring at each other as folk began to take note.

"Just a joke to you two, ent I?" Raddock demanded. "Square Girls' Club, laughing at Raddock behind his back while you . . . you . . ." His face screwed up in disgust.

"Ent like that, Raddock," Deardra said. "Wanted Selia to marry you as much as any."

"So you could keep her close?" Raddock demanded. "Shame me whenever I wasn't about?"

"Ever think for a ripping second that maybe the world don't revolve around Raddock Fisher?" Selia asked. "Ent so much as brought me flowers, but I'm supposed to fall into your arms because your da talked to mine? Did you ever spare a moment to consider what I might want?"

"I was supposed to guess what you wanted was my sister?"

Deardra crossed her arms. "Not anymore. Harl din't tell all. She's cast us both aside for Anjy Watch."

❧

Selia and Anjy sat at opposite sides of her father's table, Jeorje and Edwar between them, facing each other across the polished wood. Neither of the men sat.

Raddock could have shouted the news far and wide. It was market day, and the whole town would have known by sunset. But that would have shamed him, as well. Instead he marched right to Jeorje, who was helping oversee work on the schoolhouse.

"Apologies, Square, for bringing this . . . indecency into your house." Jeorje's face was stone.

"You didn't bring anything," Selia said.

Jeorje looked at her as though she were a disobedient toddler throwing a tantrum, then turned back to Edwar. "Seems your girl didn't need much prodding, but that doesn't mean I don't share responsibility for bringing temptation to your borough." He turned a hard glare at Anjy. Her eyes were down, but she wilted under the weight of it, nevertheless. "Thought my granddaughter and I had an understanding about how she was to behave here, but the Canon reminds us wickedness runs deep. Time she was back under my roof, where I can keep my eye on her and the switch to hand."

Edwar spread his hands, trying to put everyone at

ease. "No real harm done here, Watch. Just girls . . ."—he shrugged—"experimenting."

It was the wrong thing to say. "Experimenting!" Jeorje shouted. "Two marriages ruined, and you call it experimenting! These are women grown, Square, not children who ent been taught better!"

"Then why are you talking to each other and not to us?" Selia demanded. Jeorje threw her that look, but she rose from her seat, giving it back tenfold. "Anjy didn't ruin my marriage to Raddock. Neither did Deardra. I'm not marrying Raddock because I don't want to."

Jeorje pursed his lips, turning back to Edwar. "Heard it right from her lips. Girls don't know what they want."

"We're women grown until we disagree with you," Selia noted, "then back to girls. I've always known what I want, and it ent Raddock Fisher."

"Well, it won't be my granddaughter, I can tell you." Jeorje reached for his hat. "Come along, girl."

Anjy said nothing, eyes still on the floor, but she rose and followed meekly after her grandfather. Selia reached for her as she passed, but Edwar caught her arm, shaking his head.

Lory blew out a breath when the door shut behind them, turning to Selia. "Why didn't you just tell us?"

"How could I," Selia asked, "when you keep telling me it's time to start a family?"

Lory put her fists on her hips. "Don't put this on me, girl. Ent the Creator to see all. But you also ent the first young woman who'd rather kiss girls than boys. Doesn't mean you need to give up on children and family."

"Just on happiness," Selia said.

"There's more to happiness than kissing," Lory said. "Night, half the time it gets in the way."

Edwar spread his hands. "Don't think that's helping, Lory. Might be best we let this sit for a night. Talk again on the morrow."

"What does it matter?" Selia pushed away from the table. "There's nothing to talk about. I'm going to market."

"Are you sure that's a good idea?" Lory asked.

Selia shrugged. "Hiding here ent going to fill the bread box. Either everyone knows, and we'll need to face it, or no one knows, and we'd best act normal."

It seemed the latter, as Selia walked the stalls. Folk greeted her warmly, filling her basket with bread, milk and cheese, fresh fruits and vegetables, with nary a word for recompense. The Speaker and schoolmam's family were always provided for by the townsfolk.

She found herself wandering to Bil Square's stall, but neither he nor his mother were there. She was about to turn away when she heard a thump and a grunt from behind the stall. Selia hurried around to see Bil on the ground, clutching his stomach, Raddock Fisher standing over him.

"What's going on here?" Selia demanded.

"Told him what would happen," Raddock said. "What is it about town that turns folk square? First Bil, then you and my filthy sister, now Anjy Watch. Pretty girl like that ought to have suitors lined up. Instead . . ."

"Get on back to work, Bil," Selia said. Raddock moved to block his path as Bil got to his feet, but Selia interposed herself. "Me you're angry with, Raddock. Don't take it out on Bil."

Raddock looked at her and blew out a breath. "Don't need to be like this, Selia. Only a few folk know"—he turned a glare on Bil, who shrank back—"and they'll keep quiet. We can still fix this. I'll have you, even now."

"*Have* me?" Selia demanded. "Like I'm some cow with sour milk you'll take out of the goodness of your heart? Get it through your head, Raddock. I. Don't. Want. You."

Raddock glared and balled his bandaged fist. Selia readied herself. This was all his fault. Thinking she was something he could possess, like her hand was owed to him. It was Raddock's fault Deardra kept her at arm's length. Raddock's fault Anjy was gone. She hoped he would take a swing at her, so she could at least have the satisfaction of blacking his eye.

But whether he saw all that in her eyes, or simply thought better of trying to hit the Speaker's daughter, Raddock took a step back, shaking his fist instead of swinging it.

"You were never a prize, Selia. Face like stone and paps like flatcakes. Da's money and station were what made you worth marrying. Word gets out, doubt even that'll be enough."

Selia slapped him, a loud retort that knocked him back. Anger and humiliation splayed across Raddock's reddening face. He put a hand to it and hurried out of the marketplace.

"You all right?" Selia asked Bil.

"Was about to ask you," Bil said. "Folk found out about you and Deardra?"

"You knew?" Selia asked. Night, maybe the whole town did know.

Bil shrugged. "See things, when you look girls in the eye instead of the bubbies. Don't think anyone else knows. You want, you can use me."

"Use you?" Selia put her hands on her hips. What new nonsense was this?

"Keep your secret," Bil said. "Folk see us walking, think you turned down Raddock because you wanted someone else."

Selia smiled, laying a hand on his shoulder. "Kind of you, Bil, but we both deserve better than that."

3

The Hive

334 AR

Jeph Bales blew out a breath, looking flushed. "Never would've guessed that in a hundred years, but it explains a lot."

"Yes," Selia said, "and no. Raddock had a swollen head and Jeorje had a harsh view of folk who were different long before my . . . indiscretions."

"That why you never . . ." Jeph trailed off at the glare Selia gave him, waving weakly at Selia's belly.

"Don't see that's your business, Jeph Bales," Selia said.

Jeph was quick to nod. "Ay, Speaker. Sorry."

"Time we were going, in any event," Selia said. "Wasted enough of your night with storytelling, but folk are going to talk, and it was best you heard it from me."

Meada put a hand on her shoulder, squeezing.

"Dun't sound like you done anythin' wrong, Speaker," Brine said. His eyes lingered a moment on Lesa Square, the lone member of the Square militia Selia brought into Jeph's common for her tale.

"Ay, well," Selia said. "Ent the whole story, but it's all you're getting tonight."

Her militia was waiting outside, armed and alert as they escorted her back to town. Word would spread soon enough. Fifty years was a long time, but there were still a few in the Brook who remembered what happened next, and the rumors that went along with it.

Selia left Lesa with the militia in the square, riding home alone with memories that had haunted her for fifty years. She wanted nothing but her bed, but instead she found Lesa waiting in the darkness on the porch.

"Go home, girl," Selia said.

"Mam and Da are still camped at Jeph's." Lesa moved to follow Selia into the house.

Selia turned, blocking the entrance. "Ay, maybe. But I'm tired, Lesa."

Lesa smirked. "Always say that, until I—"

"Not tonight." Selia tried to close the door, but Lesa shoved her foot in the frame.

"Don't care what happened fifty years ago, Selia. This ent then, and we ent promised to anyone."

Selia reached out, gently putting a hand on Lesa's shoulder. The girl tried to lean in, but Selia shoved her back instead. She stumbled and caught herself on the porch rail. "Woodbrained girl. Ent told you how it ended."

Lesa stepped forward, and Selia slammed the door in her face, dropping the bar.

Then she put her back to it, slid to the floor, and wept.

❧

Sleep was harder to find than usual. Selia paced the house till nearly dawn, lost in memories fifty years in the past. When she finally crawled into bed, it seemed her eyes barely closed before a loud rap on her door startled her awake.

"Fool girl," Selia muttered, seeing light streaming through the window. "Wants the whole town to see her." She pulled on a dressing gown and went to the door as the rapping continued.

She lifted the bar and yanked the door open. "Enough!"

Mack Pasture's young grandson Tam took a step back at her shout, eyes wide. "Sorry, Speaker. Din't think you were asleep. Midmorning."

Selia glanced at the sky and saw he was right. She'd slept more than she thought. "Everything all right?"

"Ent," Tam said. "Da says you need to hurry. Corelings're actin' . . . strange."

Selia's eyes narrowed. "Strange, how?"

"Up to something in the woods," Tam said. "Heard the noise all night. Crashes and cracks, like a crew of Cutters clearing a stand."

"Night," Selia said, remembering Renna Tanner's warning. "Come in and tell me everything." She led him to the kitchen table, pushing the cookie crock his way while she put the kettle on.

❦

Selia sent Tam up Boggin's Hill to the Holy House, where Tender Harral blew a signal on the great horn. Less than an hour later, Selia's militia was mustered in the square.

"What's happened?" Lucik asked as Selia rode up, armor and weapons strapped to her horse.

"Trouble up on Mack Pasture's land. Just going for a look now, but expect fighting tonight. Want a warded camp set up in his fallow field."

"Ay, Speaker." Lucik turned and went to give the orders.

Lesa approached next. "Get your rest?"

Selia heard the bitterness in the words, and took a

deep breath, blowing it out slowly through her nostrils. "Slept like a babe. Sounds like the Pastures had a rougher night. Mount up. I want to be at his farm before we lose the afternoon."

Selia could see the young woman was stung by the dismissal, but there was nothing for it. Daylight was wasting.

The Cutters met them on the road and Selia set a hard pace that had them at Mack's farm by midafternoon, but not fast enough, it seemed.

The Watches beat her there.

"Should've worn my armor," Selia muttered, seeing Jeorje Watch talking to Mack while his men hobbled horses and set up wardposts in the field she'd meant for her own fighters.

"What's that, Speaker?" Lucik asked.

"Just grumbles." Selia slipped down from her horse, leaving her spear and shield behind with her armor.

Sometimes a straight back's as good as armor, her da used to say, and Selia took the advice, striding right up to Mack and Jeorje. "Pasture. Speaker."

"Speaker." Mack nodded. "Thank you for coming so quickly."

"Selia." Jeorje's head barely tilted as he deliberately left off her title.

As ever, Selia was forced to ignore the slight. It would cost more face to correct him than to let it slide, as Jeorje well knew. "What's happened?"

"Demons came out in force last night," Mack said.

"Happens on new moon." Selia's eyes passed over Mack's farmhouse, barns, day pens, and fields. "Doesn't look like they did much damage."

"Din't attack the wards," Mack said. "Like I was tellin' Jeorje, they stayed out in the woods. Heard crashes and bangs all night. Could see the glow of fire, smell smoke. Up to something, Selia. Bet the farm on it."

"Ent gone for a look since sunup?" Selia asked.

Mack swallowed hard. "Figured it was best to wait for the militia. Dark in those woods."

Selia snorted. "Little shade ent dark enough for demons, Pasture."

"Did the right thing," Jeorje said, if only to contradict her. He laid a hand on Mack's shoulder. "We'll get to the bottom of this."

Despite her chiding of Mack, Selia took the time to fetch her weapons and armor before heading into the woods with Brine and Lucik while the militia made an uncomfortable camp next to the Watchmen.

As Mack had claimed, there were signs of felled trees everywhere. Cracked stumps, deep holes, flinders of wood and roots jutting from the torn soil like broken bones. Of the trees themselves, there was little sign.

"Night," Lucik said.

"Ent normal, Selia," Brine said. "Mack's got the right of that."

They found Jeorje deeper in the woods, squatting in front of a wide trench and running his hand over the bank. It was shallow, perhaps a yard deep in most places, but it ran in both directions, curving around out of sight.

"Soil's fresh," Jeorje said, examining the dirt on his fingers with a sniff. "This was dug last night, and then packed smooth." He turned to Brine. "Ever see a demon clean its own mess, Cutter?"

"Ent." Brine was a giant of a man, but he shuddered, eyes roving the surrounding trees as if expecting wood demons to drop down from the boughs at any moment. "What do you make of it, Selia?"

Selia pursed her lips, walking along the edge of the trench, following its curves with her eyes. "They're building a greatward, just like on Jeph's farm."

Even Jeorje looked up at that. "Surely not."

Selia blew out a breath, continuing to walk the lines, more certain with every moment. "Arlen Bales told his da something like this happened in Hollow County on new moon. Means a coreling prince has come to Tibbet's Brook."

Lucik's eyes grew wide. "Demons got royalty?"

"No more than hornets," Selia said, "but that don't mean we want 'em building a nest. Brine, I want Cutters up in the trees. Now. See if you can map it out."

"Ay, Speaker."

"You and Jeph Bales been keepin' secrets." Jeorje's jaw was tight. He didn't like that there were things she knew that he didn't. "Messenger didn't trust the council with any of this."

"Any reason he should've?" Selia asked. "Had it your way, his promised would be in a demon's belly."

Jeorje looked to be chewing his own cheek. "Ent one to talk, Selia."

Stung, Selia had no retort. She sighed. What was the point of arguing now? Jeorje had a right to know what they were facing.

"Mind demons, they're called. Only come out three nights a month—new moon and the nights before and after. Pinch your thoughts like stealing an apple from a cart, you're not careful. Make sure your men have mind wards on their helmets."

"Saw to that already," Jeorje said. "Anything about how to kill 'em, or what this demon ward does?"

"Expect it's like our wards. Meant to keep us out once

night falls. We let the corelings finish it, they can work more mischief in succor. As for how to kill them . . ." Selia shrugged. "Put a spear in 'em, I reckon."

Brine's Cutters scaled trees easy as climbing a ladder, shouting and pointing to something deeper in the woods. Selia and Jeorje went to investigate, pulling up short as they found the missing lumber.

"Night," Selia said.

"Creator protect us," Jeorje added, drawing a ward in the air.

The trees had been hauled to the center of the demon ward, arranged like twigs in a dome that had the appearance of a gigantic weaver bird's nest, packed with dirt from the trenches. Shielded from the sun, its entrance was dark and forbidding.

"Ent goin' in there, day or not," Brine said.

"Honest word," Lucik agreed.

"Can we burn it?" Selia asked.

Brine put a hand against the structure, trying not to let the others see his fingers shaking. "Damp soil. Raw wood. Maybe if we had time, but," he looked up at the dim light filtering through the trees, "runnin' out of sun."

"Wardposts," Selia said. "Circle that nest. Make sure the mind wards are biggest. If a coreling prince has come to the Brook, you can bet the farm it's in there."

"Ent going to matter, that demon ward lights up," Jeorje noted.

"Could we fill the trenches?" Lucik asked.

"If we put every hand on it," Jeorje said, "we might do in a few months."

Selia shook her head. "We can't undo the demons' work, but we can mar it." She pointed to the map. "Here and here. Lucik, have men with spades collapse the banks. Brine, have Cutters fell trees to fall across the trenches."

"Ay," Brine said.

"What good will that do?" Mack demanded. "Corelings will just come haul them away."

"Ay," Selia agreed. "And we'll be waiting."

☙

"They'll be risin' soon," Selia called to her fighters. "Everyone remember why we're here. We keep the ward from activating at all cost. Do not let the demons work."

This is a terrible idea. Selia gripped her spear in a sweaty fist as she dropped into the shallow trench and hunched down. It was barely waist-high—she could leap clear in an instant—but it was still hard to shake the feeling of being cornered. Trapped.

It didn't help that Jeorje Watch knelt a few feet away, face serene as he prayed, his walking stick laid across his knees. He'd gone along with Selia's plans, acting as if they were his all along, but he wouldn't allow her the glory of holding the front line alone.

And so they waited as the shadows lengthened and full dark fell. Selia's breath hissed as the rising began, corelings drifting like smoke from the ground. Jeorje's eyes popped open, scanning the trench floor, but demons couldn't rise through worked surfaces, and the hard-packed soil of the trench seemed sufficient to push them up the bank. A wood demon began to materialize right above Jeorje. It was at its most vulnerable at this moment, but he took his time, making sure he did not ruin their surprise. Then he gave a signal, echoed down the line among his men. They readied weapons as he unsheathed the spearpoint at the end of his cane, then drove it like a stake up through the demon's belly into its black heart.

Magic crackled along the cane like lectricity drawn to

a lightning rod, and Selia could well imagine the rush of
power he felt.

"Now!" she cried, picking her own target, a wood demon materializing a few feet away atop the trench bank.
She straightened to her full six-foot height, coming up
from hiding to drive her spear into the coreling's back.
The warded head punched through scale and hide, drinking deep of the demon's magic and turning it into killing
power. Only a fraction of that energy fed back into her, but
it was enough to fill her with a mad strength. She yanked
the demon down into the trench, Lucik and Lesa putting
spears into it as well. It gave a final thrash, and lay still.

Selia had her shield up now, moving north along the
trench with her fighters as Jeorje moved south. Demons
that had materialized away from the trench raced their
way, but Brine and his Cutters roared from the trees,
hacking at them from behind.

There were shrieks and flashes of wardlight from
deeper in the woods, as demons attempted to exit the
nest, only to find it surrounded by wardposts that kept
them pinned.

Selia's eyes swept ahead, seeing a ten-foot-tall rock demon around the next bend of the trench. The beast looked
confused, expecting to dig rather than do battle, but it
was more than willing as Selia and her fighters rounded
the bend.

The rock demon swiped its great talons at her, but
the wards on Selia's angled shield deflected the blow. She
planted her feet and weathered the impact as she stabbed
with her spear. The demon had greater reach, but she
managed to poke its arm before it retracted. Piercing
wards flared and the demon roared from the sting, but it
was a minor blow that failed to penetrate its thick cara-
pace.

It swiped again with its other arm, but Lesa was there, putting her shoulder behind her shield to cover Selia. The demon tried to spin, swiping at them with its great tail, but the narrow trench tripped it up and, as it stumbled, they struck hard. Lesa stabbed into the joint of the demon's armored knee, buckling the limb and allowing Selia a clear strike at the gap between the plates in the demon's groin.

The demon fell their way, but the women danced back, steps in sync like a festival reel. They parted and Lucik rushed between them, planting his spear into the demon's eye.

It was a killing blow, but even in its death throes a rock demon was dangerous. One of its flailing arms caught Lucik against the trench wall. Her senses alive with magic, Selia heard the sound of bone breaking.

"Lucik!" She bulled in, heedless of the danger. The demon had stopped thrashing, but Lucik was trapped by its bulk, face reddening. Selia stuck her spear between the demon and tunnel wall like a lever.

"Get him out! He can't breathe!" She grit her teeth and put her back against the spear, bracing against the wall with both feet. She screamed, straining against the rock's weight as Lesa ran in, dragging Lucik free.

"He all right?" Selia asked when she extricated herself.

"I'm . . ." Lucik's breath was labored, ". . . fine . . . Speaker . . ."

"Good boy, Lucik, but you ent fine. Out of this fight."

"Just . . ." Lucik tried to put a hand under himself, " . . . need a minute for the magic to set me right."

There was a low growl, and Selia looked up to see a field demon crouching on the lip of the trench. "Ent got a minute."

Lesa tried to get her shield up as the coreling pounced,

but it was too fast, knocking her sprawling. Her spear bounced out of reach and one of the straps on her shield snapped, causing it to hang awkwardly from her arm, a poor defense. The smaller wards on her armor sparked and flared as the demon's claws scrabbled across them, but they dimmed as she and the demon rolled on the trench floor, dirt gumming the etchings.

"Lesa!" Selia cried, rushing in, but she could not find a clear target to stab without risk of hitting Lesa as they struggled.

The demon's claws found purchase at last, tearing armor plate like paper as its jaws snapped forward at Lesa's bared throat. Selia abandoned her own spear and shield to tackle the demon, knocking it off Lesa. Selia landed atop the creature, the impact blowing the breath from its lungs. Her heavy gloves were reinforced with warded steel across the knuckles, and there was a thunderclap as she punched the wriggling demon in the face.

Ground and pound, her father used to call the move. Selia pressed warded greaves into the demon's lower limbs, keeping it pinned as she fell into her breath, hammering it with punch after punch. Each blow leached a little more magic from the beast, making the next one stronger as her momentum built. Again and again she struck, blowing a breath from her mouth with each punch and sucking a fresh one through her nose on each recoil.

"Selia." The voice was distant and she ignored it. Nothing mattered but hammering the demon. The world fell away, and there was only the struggle for survival.

"SELIA!" Lesa screamed, grabbing her shoulder. Selia turned on the girl, magic burning through her limbs, and nearly punched her head off.

Lesa saw the blow coming and parried it, rushing in

to wrap Selia in her arms. "All right now, Selia. It's dead.
It's dead."

Selia stared at the ichor-spattered demon beneath her,
its head a ruined mass. Only then did she let out a shuddering breath, returning Lesa's embrace.

"You almost died." Selia's vision blurred as she began
to weep. "And I was so awful to you, the last time we—"

"Shhh," Lesa whispered, kissing her. "It's all right.
Just Old Lady Barren tryin' to scare me off. But I don't
scare easy."

"Thank the Creator." Selia returned the kiss, then
caught sight of Lucik Boggin, staring at them, eyes wide.

"Got something to say, boy?"

Lucik immediately dropped his eyes. "No, Speaker."

"Good boy."

☙

The demon ranks thinned after the initial assault, and the
militias were able to hold the trenches until the sky began to lighten. When the remaining demons began to mist
back down to the Core, Selia finally put up her spear and
blew out a breath.

"Creator be praised." Jeorje sheathed the tip of his
cane and turned to his great-nephew Fredd Watch. "Send
runners to Southwatch and Soggy Marsh. I want every
strong back in town up here first thing in the morning,
taking this ward apart."

"Ay, Speaker." Fredd punched a fist to his chest and
ran off.

Selia's mouth was sour, but she turned to Brine. "He's
right. Fishers, Boggins, Baleses, Pastures. We need every
hand on this. Caught 'em with their breeches down to-

night, but don't reckon that trick will work twice, and there's still one night left to new moon."

"An' next month?" Brine asked. "Month after that?"

Selia spread her hands. "Core if I know. For now, take the wounded back to camp in Mack's field, and see if we can get Coline Trigg up here."

"Ay, Speaker," Brine said.

Lesa met her eyes as Brine stepped away, and Selia felt her breath catch. Jeorje had a bride at home no older than Lesa. His seventh. Yet she was denying herself?

"Reckon Mack's got an empty hayloft, girl?"

The smile that broke across Lesa's face brightened the twilight. "Ay, think we can find a spot."

Jeorje's eyes followed the two women as they walked away, but Selia ignored it. Jeorje wasn't the only one whose winters had turned to summers. If she was being given another chance at life, she didn't mean to let Jeorje Watch and Raddock Fisher dictate how it was lived.

❧

The whole town lent a hand after sunup, marring the demon greatward by felling trees, paring brush, and digging furrows to break the lines. Mack and his family were given warded weapons, and teams were sent to search the woods for any sign the demons had begun work elsewhere.

The Marshes arrived around midday, grim-faced as they drove several carts heavily laden with barrels into the camp.

"What's this?" Selia asked.

"A condition of our compact," Jeorje said. "For too long, the Marshes have drowned their problems, wallowing in strong drink rather than solving with hard work."

Selia couldn't argue. Soggy Marsh was famed for its stills, producing marsh water, a spirit made from fermented rice that could double as lamp oil. Marsh water wasn't as tasty as Boggin's ale, but Hog did a brisk business selling it in the General Store. Two fingers were enough to put smaller folk off balance. Four could set a grown man stumbling about, singing half-forgotten songs at the top of his lungs.

"This solves two problems at once," Jeorje said.

"The hive," Selia said.

Jeorje nodded to Keven Marsh as the young man gave a respectful bow. "All here, Speaker. Every barrel in the Marsh."

"No doubt some folk have hidden a bit away, but we'll find it in time," Jeorje said.

They led the carts to the great demon hive, Marshes hauling casks up to the top and cracking them open while others worked a fire pump, spraying the logs and mud with marsh water.

When the last of it was dumped, the stink of alcohol was thick in the air. Jeorje himself lit the torch and threw it into the pile, reading from the Canon as the hive burned, sending great billowing clouds of evil black smoke into the sky.

The Marshes watched sadly as their beloved marsh water burned. The heat and smoke made their eyes water, tears streaking the greasy ash on their faces.

There were shrieks within as the hive dome collapsed. An hour later the structure imploded, falling in on itself and leaving a crater of frightening depth beneath. Yawning tunnels circled the crater in almost every direction, illuminated by the burning wreckage. All stretched deep into the ground, farther than Selia could see.

"All the way to the Core, or I'm a Fisher." Brine shuddered.

☙

They were on guard as the sun set—hundreds of spears, mattocks, and bows—but there was no sign of corelings rising as full dark came.

"Not so much as a Regular," Selia told the other Speakers.

"Maybe they ran off for good?" Lucik ventured hopefully.

"These demon princes are as clever as you say, they know we're waiting," Jeorje said. "They—"

Everyone's head turned as the great horn sounded, counting the blasts. Four long, and one short. Selia saw smoke and the glow of fire.

The corelings had attacked Fishing Hole.

☙

"What if it's a trap?" Lesa asked. "Lurin' us away so they can get back to work on the hive?"

"Ent a gamble I'm willing to make with all Fishing Hole on the table." Selia banged her spear against her mended shield. "Saddle up! Fishers need our help!"

They raced across the Brook, heedless of the moonless night. Selia set a brutal pace that many of the others, traveling on foot or less experienced at riding, could not maintain, but Jeorje's great gray stallion matched her gelding stride for stride. Selia could not tell if that was due to concern for the Fishers, or a refusal to be seen as second to her.

Arrogant, idiot woman, she cursed herself. *What does it matter? Knew these demons were smart. Knew their sights were set on the Brook. But you had to keep your grudges. Now the Fishers are going to pay for it.*

Selia hated herself in that moment, hated her lifetime of failures. Anjy Watch. Renna Tanner. Core take her if every man, woman, and child in Fishing Hole was added to that list.

There were houses aflame when they thundered over the bridge into Fishing Hole. Some folk had taken to the water to escape the blaze, their vessels outlined in firelight and the flare of wards as water demons sought to pull them under. Human remains were scattered in the street, but screams told Selia it was not too late for most of the folk.

Something stumbled into their path, forcing Selia and Jeorje to pull up so hard they nearly lost their seats. They had weapons ready, but it was only Raddock Lawry, clutching a head wound that matted his hair and beard with blood. "Speaker!"

"Raddock." Selia lowered her spear. "What—"

Before she could finish the words, Raddock swept an arm their way, the limb growing into a sinuous tentacle with a great hooked talon bigger than a reaping scythe at its end. The claw whipped across, severing the front legs of their horses like barley stalks.

Butter let out a horrific cry, crashing into the mud. Selia tried to throw herself free, but was caught and pinned as the animal rolled atop her.

Jeorje was quicker, leaping from the saddle and keeping his feet as his stallion went down. The demon's taloned limb whipped again, cracking across his head. The strap of his steel-reinforced hat broke and he hit the ground hard, walking stick bouncing out of reach.

Butter continued to thrash, momentarily taking the weight off Selia. She tried to pull free, but the horse fell back again, blasting the breath from her lungs and smashing her face-first into the mud. She came up spitting as Butter screamed and twisted again. This time she managed to scramble away, wiping mud from her eyes.

The coreling wearing Raddock's form was rushing her. Lesa threw her spear at it, but the demon threw itself back, sinuous as a snake as it dodged the spear and whipped back upright, barely losing momentum.

Jeorje recovered his weapon, stalking in on the demon. It lashed at him again but the old Watchman batted the blow aside, coming in quick. He raised his cane for a blow, but instead gave a bellow of pain, dropping the weapon and clutching at his head. He fell to his knees, thrashing and screaming.

Selia spat another mouthful of mud, grasping for the slippery shaft of her spear. She found it and turned to face the coreling.

But then she felt it. A presence in her mind, setting every nerve in her body aflame as easily as she might turn up the wick of a lamp. She tried to resist, understanding that it was not real pain, but it made no difference in the sensation. Muscles spasmed and she found herself screaming.

Memories began to flash unbidden across her mind's eye, the demon rolling back the years like flipping pages in a journal. Some it passed without consideration—moments of joy, or pride, or happiness. The coreling lingered instead on failures. Pains. Her weakest, most helpless moments. The burning of the school. The staking of Renna Tanner. Weeping on the road to Sunny Pasture, covered in blood.

Tears streaked the mud on her face. She could hear fighting as the militia thundered across the bridge, but it was a distant thing, like folk laughing on a porch down the road.

The demon probed deeper, delving into thoughts so precious, so private, that Selia instinctively raged in response. Her anger seemed to give the coreling pause and, in that moment, she felt something. A tingling on her forehead.

The mind ward, Selia realized. It was still there, on her helmet, covered in mud that kept it from functioning properly.

She reached for it, but there was resistance in the air, as though she were pushing her hand into a rice barrel. She grit her teeth, clumsily swiping at the mud on her helmet.

The moment she did, the resistance lessened. She could still feel the presence in her mind, but it was weaker now as the ward gained power. Selia stuck her muddy hand into a seam in her armor, searching. After several frantic moments she pulled free a kerchief, using it to wipe the helmet clean.

Immediately the pressure in her mind ceased, the fire running across her nerves snuffed like a candle. Her vision cleared and she saw the demon changeling feathered with arrows, their warded heads glowing angrily beneath its flesh. The thing with Raddock's face gave an inhuman shriek and melted away, leaving the arrows lying in the mud as it re-formed into a field demon and fled the continuing fire.

"Secure the streets!" Selia stumbled to her feet, moving to Jeorje, who continued to writhe on the ground clutching at his head. She found his hat, banded with steel, etched with mind wards.

She moved close to place it back on Jeorje's head, but

he curled and sprang at her suddenly, wrapping his powerful arms around her legs and twisting her to the ground.

"Jeorje! Get hold of yourself!" Selia didn't wait to see if the words got through, punching hard against his unprotected head.

Jeorje accepted the blow, using his greater weight to pin her to the ground, hands at her throat. "Should've rid this town of you fifty years ago."

"This . . . ent . . . you . . ." Selia gasped the words, pulling helplessly at Jeorje's wrists as he choked her. Her feet thrashed and kicked, but she could not get them under her to force him off or reverse the pin. She managed to slam a knee between his legs, but even that only seemed to intensify the mad look in Jeorje's eyes.

Selia's vision began to blur. Lesa was screaming her name, but demons were pouring out of Fishing Hole, and it was all the militia could do to hold them back.

Balling a steel-gauntleted fist, Selia put the last of her strength into a shallow right hook into the back of Jeorje's elbow. The blow hyperextended the joint, and for a moment his grip weakened.

Selia drew a rasping breath and punched again, hitting Jeorje in the throat. It was his turn to gasp then, as Selia curled her legs up and kicked out, knocking him back. "Corespawn it!" Her voice was a hoarse rasp. "It ent you! It's the demon!"

But was it really? Perhaps a coreling prince was nudging his mind, but no doubt this was a fantasy Jeorje had nursed for decades in the dark corners of his heart.

"Murderer!" He came at her again.

This time Selia was ready, slipping his punch and coming in underneath, hooking him in the ribs, right, left, and right again before quick-stepping away. His prideful refusal to wear proper armor was a weakness here. There were plates between the layers of his coat, but it was open in the front, and she was able to snake through. Even in his madness, Jeorje could not easily shrug off the heavy blows from her reinforced fists.

He tried to grapple again, and this time Selia accepted the hold, grabbing his shoulders and pulling him down even as her armored knee came up to meet his kidney. She shoved him back, stunned, and he was unable to dodge a side kick that put him on the ground.

He put his hands under him, and Selia knew the battle was far from over. Instead of attacking or moving to retreat, she snatched up his hat and thrust it down on his head.

Jeorje shook his head, the madness leaving his eyes as he looked up at her. "Selia, what . . . ?"

"Demon was in your mind," Selia said. "Touched mine, as well."

Jeorje's mouth was a flat line as he got to his feet, turning his eyes to scan the street.

"You're welcome," Selia said at his back.

Jeorje pretended not to hear the words, retrieving his spear-tipped cane. "Doesn't change things, Selia."

Selia let it go at that, picking up her own spear and shield. The words were as close to thanks as she was going to get. The two of them readied to join the battle, only to find it fading. The demons, so numerous a moment ago, were scattering into the night.

They swept the streets of Fishing Hole, finding survivors everywhere. Under the direction of a coreling prince, the demons had penetrated the wards almost effortlessly, but they seemed more interested in drawing the Brook's leaders into a trap than in killing Fishers. The real Raddock had taken refuge on one of the fishing boats.

"This is your fault," Raddock snarled when he made it back to shore. "Protection, you promised, yet you leave my borough without means to defend itself, and take all your fighters to protect one Pasture's farm?"

What he'd said wasn't entirely fair, but neither was he wrong. It had been a mistake to withhold fighting wards from the Fishers, no matter what they'd done. She opened her mouth to reply.

"You speak honest word, Fisher," Jeorje cut in before Selia could speak. He put a hand out. "Southwatch can help you rebuild, and see your fishing spears warded before the next new moon."

Raddock stared at the hand for a long moment, then reached out and took it. He glared at Selia as the men shook.

Had that comin'.

&

Town Square bustled over the next fortnight. Selia had people bending their backs sunrise to sunset, pulling up the paving stones in the square and re-laying them in a mosaic warding. Scared folk took on debt in Hog's ledgers at the General Store for tools and supplies to help them construct their own greatwards. The tavern was equally busy, Marshes bitterly drinking Boggin's ale as everyone shared their fears.

Watchmen passed through in numbers, heading to Fishing Hole with laden carts of lumber and supplies. Jeorje was making good on his promise, and Selia couldn't bring herself to condemn it. She'd had all the time in the world to make things right with the Fishers.

Selia was everywhere in town, soothing nerves and

turning them into productivity. The demons had not re-
sumed work on the hive, but there was little that could be
done to fill the massive pit, and none were fool enough to
venture into its tunnels.

Lesa began staying openly at her house, ostensibly as her
assistant, but it seemed folk had been asking their elders,
as Raddock bid. The two of them drew looks whenever
folk thought they weren't watching, and some normally
friendly faces were . . . colder. Still, none challenged them
openly, and Selia began to think Lesa had been right.

"Mam asked if I was a square girl today," Lesa told
Selia one night.

There was a rattle, and Selia saw her hand shaking the
cup in its saucer. She set it on the table before she spilled
her tea. "What did you say?"

"Honest word," Lesa said.

Selia drew a deep breath. "And still she let you come
back here?"

"Woman grown, even if Old Lady Barren don't want
to see it," Lesa said. "Mam don't get to 'let' me do anything."

Selia nodded. "Fair and true. What did she say?"

"What I expected," Lesa said. "Loves me, and ent gonna
stop. You're a good woman who's done right by this town,
but older'n me, and we won't always see eye to eye. Sad I
won't have children."

Selia instinctively touched her own belly, pretending to
smooth her dress. "Ways around that, we want."

Lesa put her hands on her hips. "Ent gonna let some
man—"

Selia silenced her with a wave. "Don't need him to
touch you. Like basting a roast. Pastures do it all the time
with livestock."

Lesa made a face and Selia laughed, kissing her. The weight she'd carried for years was finally lifting. She went to bed with an easy heart.

And woke in the morning to the sound of the Messenger horn.

❦

Though he brought no goods and only a small letter satchel, folk clustered in the tavern as the Messenger met the town council in the back room of Hog's store. His armor was freshly scratched and dented, man and mount haggard from the journey. He had dark hair and beard, with eyes like a nightwolf.

"My name is Marick." The man held up his satchel, sealed with a mortar and pestle crest. "I come as a representative of Mistress Leesha Paper, Countess of Hollow County."

"Countess is a Gatherer?" Coline asked in surprise.

"Ay," Marick said. "And thank the Creator for it. There was none better to lead when the Krasians came."

"Krasians came out of the desert?" Hog asked.

Marick nodded. "Made war on the Free Cities. Conquered Fort Rizon, and took the mainland in Lakton, driving refugees north in the thousands."

"Creator." Harral drew a ward in the air.

"An alliance between Miln and Angiers stopped their advance," Marick said. "That . . . and the common enemy."

"Corelings," Selia said.

Marick handed her his satchel. "It's all there in Mistress Leesha's letter, Speaker. Demons are swarming, looking to build new hives all over Thesa."

Selia nodded. "Seen their handiwork already. Marred their greatward in the western woods and set the hive ablaze. Left with a honeycomb we reckon leads all the way to the Core."

"Night," Marick said. "Did you see the mind demon?"

"No, but I felt it in my head before I got my wards in place." Selia didn't mention Jeorje had been invaded, as well. Now more than ever, they needed unity.

"Luckier than you know, Speaker," Marick said. "Ent many get that close and walk away. But you need to understand, it ent over. They'll be back next month, stronger than ever. Hatchling queen takes residence in that hive, she'll see your town as her personal larder."

"What can we do?" Brine asked.

The Messenger shrugged. "Your home, your decision. Want my advice? Pack up and leave town before next new moon."

❧

Lesa left the house the next morning to help train recruits for the militia. On one thing, Selia and Jeorje were in agreement. They would be corespawned before they abandoned Tibbet's Brook to the corelings.

A moment later, there was a knock at the door. Selia answered to find Tender Harral wringing his hands and looking decidedly uncomfortable.

Selia tsked. "How long were you waiting, hoping she'd leave?"

"Long enough," Harral said.

Selia sighed and opened the door wider. "Might as well come in before she gets back. I'll put a fresh kettle on."

"Thank you," Harral said.

"Stewert never told you I was a square girl?" Selia asked. "Night, *the* square girl?"

Harral shook his head. "Tender Stewert, Creator rest

his spirit, died well before his time. Perhaps he meant to, when I was older."

Indeed, Harral had been an acolyte barely in his twenties when his master died, leaving him Tender to seven hundred folk, not counting Southwatch. He'd stumbled in the beginning, but found wisdom in later years. Selia held out hope it extended to this.

"Selia—" Harral began.

"Creator made me, same as you," Selia cut in. "Must've had a reason why He made me see boys as friends and girls as—"

Harral held up a hand, forestalling her, but she pressed. "Can't even hear the words? Doesn't bode well, Tender."

"I know you, Selia," Harral said. "Know your heart. Know how you look to the folk of this town like your own children. That's why I've come. Make sure you've thought this through."

Selia poured the tea and set a cup in front of the Tender, not offering sugar or a cookie. "What's that supposed to mean?"

"You've fifty winters on that girl," Harral said.

"And Jeorje has ninety on his latest bride," Selia said. "Stam's got thirty on Maddy Fisher."

Harral gestured at Selia with his mug. "Ay, and Selia Speaker always judged them for it. Never approved of Jeorje taking more than one wife, or of—night—*anything* Stam Tailor does."

It was true enough, and Selia crossed her arms defensively. "Ent an excess of seventy-winter square girls in Tibbet's Brook, Tender. Magic's given me a new life. Sayin' I should spend it alone?"

Harral spread his arms, drawing attention to his plain brown robe. "Ent the only one had to give that up, Selia. Think I ent got urges? But I don't act on them, for the good of this town. Folk deserve a Holy Man who keeps his vows."

"Ay," Selia agreed. "Vows mean something. But I din't pledge my life to the Creator, Harral. What's me being alone got to do with the good of this town?"

"Folk look to you for an example," Harral said. "What's this say to them?"

"That I've a heart to love?" Selia asked. "That I ent barren, no matter what folk whisper at my back? That life's bigger'n the box we put it in?"

Harral blew out a breath. "Is your happiness worth more than Lesa's parents'?"

"They come to you?" Selia asked.

"Don't blame them, Selia," Harral said. "Only want what's best for their girl. Wanted to know what the Canon says—if she'll be denied Heaven."

"I was reading the Canon before you were born, Tender," Selia said. "Ent kind to square folk, but doesn't say we can't find Heaven."

"Ay, and that's what I told them," Harral said. "We're all the Creator's children, and it's our duty to love and stand by one another, sunrise and sunset. But—"

Selia's brows knit together. "Bein' real patient with you, Tender. Pick your next words careful."

"Folk talk, Selia," Harral said. "Word's spreading like fire through the Brook. Just rumors now, but it won't take long to confirm if you two carry on as you've done."

"Sooner the better," Selia said. "Secrets fester, and this one's had fifty years. Time it was lanced."

"Lot of folk don't approve," Harral said. "Makin' up stories about why you really stood by Renna Tanner."

Selia balled a fist. "Never laid a finger on that girl. You—"

Harral put up his hands. "Told 'em it was tampweed

talk, but I don't have to tell you folk don't always listen to their Tender. Lots standing by you, but others are grumblin', worrying about this . . . spreadin'."

"Ent a flux, Harral," Selia snapped. "It's who I am."

"We are who we choose to be, Selia," Harral said.

Selia took the cup from his hands. "Time you chose to be out of my house, then."

"Ent your enemy, Selia." Harral pushed back his chair and got to his feet. "But Raddock's got the Fishers in a stir; the Marshes are refusing to come to Town Square, and the Watches . . ."

"Know all about the Watches." Selia gave him a gentle but firm push toward the door.

"Raddock's called a council meeting," Harral said.

Selia froze. "Ay?"

"First morning of new moon," Harral said. "Says we can't afford to face it with you as Town Speaker."

❦

"Can he do that?" Lesa asked.

"Any Speaker can call a vote of no confidence," Selia said.

"Don't matter." Lesa took Selia's hand. "Folk don't like what they don't understand, but they understand Raddock Lawry turned this town upside down and got a spankin' from Arlen Bales for it. They understand you've bled for the Brook ever since. Ent no way they'll take him over you."

"Night, girl!" Selia pulled her hand away. "Ent Raddock rippin' Lawry we need to worry about. It's Jeorje."

Lesa crossed her arms. "Folk don't want to dye all their clothes black, give up ale and sugar, and go to the Holy House every day, neither."

"What they want is to not get et by corelings," Selia said. "Jeorje's got Soggy Marsh and Fishing Hole under his protection. That's half the folk in town right there. Just a few from the other boroughs vote for him . . ."

"They won't. They can't." Lesa sounded like she was trying to convince herself as much as Selia.

Selia told herself the same thing over and over in the coming days. She didn't hide that Lesa was staying in her house now, but neither did she flaunt it, keeping the girl with the others of the militia when they continued to scour the Brook at night.

But on the morning of new moon, when every fit man in Southwatch arrived in Town Square, grim-faced and with spear in hand, she knew it was already too late.

"Night," Lesa breathed.

"Can't say I'm surprised," Selia said. "Ent the first time the Watches marched into Town Square looking for a fight."

4

Far as We Need

284 AR

The Watches stopped bringing their children to Town Square on market day, but it didn't make Selia's job any easier. Without supplies and labor from Southwatch, work slowed to a crawl rebuilding the schoolhouse, and without Anjy, Raddock, and Deardra to help teach, the bulk of the extra work fell on Selia.

She took it in her stride, refusing to let problems of her making deny the children of Tibbet's Brook a proper education. She didn't know what rumors spread in Southwatch, but the rest of town acted as if nothing was amiss. The Watches had always been queer folk, prone to righteous fits, and the Fishers hadn't expected their Speaker's children to teach reading and arithmetic forever.

Selia rang the great bell, signaling the end of classes for the day. As the children filed out, Lory handed Selia a covered basket. "Jahn Messenger leaves this afternoon with his caravan. Made them butter cookies for the ride. Make sure to deliver them before you tend the shopping."

Selia took the basket, finding Jahn and her father talking amiably as the last of the Duke's rice, lumber, produce, and fish was loaded onto the carts. Jahn cut an impressive figure in his armor, polished to shine in the midday sun. Isak Fisher was with them, Raddock at his heel.

She slowed her approach, wondering if she might delay until they left, but the Messenger caught sight of her. "Selia! Come give Uncle Jahn a hug before I tread into the naked night!"

He swept Selia off her feet, and even the glares of Raddock and Isak could not keep a smile from her face. Jahn had been Edwar's apprentice long ago and was treated like family when he came to town. He crushed her to his breastplate, the smell of oil and metal and leather so like her father's that his embrace felt like home.

Jahn set her down. "Getting hard to lift you from your feet, girl. Grown tall as your father. Give good strong children to the Brook."

Isak coughed.

"Wouldn't be sure of that," Raddock grumbled.

Jahn cast an irritated glance his way. Raddock was wise enough to drop his eyes, and Jahn let it go. "Do I smell your mother's butter cookies?"

Selia excused herself quickly, wanting to be far from the Fishers. It was late afternoon, but there were still a handful of Watches in the market making last-minute purchases. A group of them noticed her and turned their backs. Creator only knew what Jeorje had told them. She drifted to another row of stalls before anyone took note.

The sight greeting her there was no better. Peat Orchard offering a shiny apple to Deardra Fisher with an exaggerated bow. ". . . almost as sweet as you."

Single young men courting Deardra, so pretty and well monied, was nothing new. But no one ever caught her attention, despite her claims of wanting a husband. Even Peat got little more than an eye roll and a patient smile— until Deardra spotted Selia.

"Always the charmer." She gave Peat a delighted laugh and her hand lingered on his as she took the fruit, giving him a kiss on the cheek. Blushing, Peat was oblivious to the self-satisfied smirk Deardra threw Selia's way.

Selia turned before Deardra could see the look on her face. It shouldn't have stung, but Deardra's betrayal couldn't dim the memories of their time together. Perhaps Deardra felt the same, and that was why she led so many boys on without a promise.

Wasn't so simple to stop being a square girl.

The day was wearing on and most folk were packing up against the coming dusk as Selia finished her rounds. She walked by Bil Square's stall to say hello, but there was only his mother Neta, haggling with Coran Marsh.

"A *barrel* of rice for a rippin' quilt?!" Coran cried. "You spin the thread from gold?"

"Quiltin's harder than havin' kids stick rice seedlings in the marsh," Neta shot back.

"Psst! Selia!" Bil hissed as Selia hurried by. He was beckoning from behind the stall, in the same secluded spot where she had confronted Raddock not long ago.

"What is it?" Selia whispered, glancing to make sure she wasn't seen before moving to join him.

She barely registered Anjy Watch before the girl threw her arms around Selia, nearly making her drop her basket. She stiffened for a moment, then fell into the embrace, holding tight and burying her face in Anjy's hair, breathing deeply of her scent.

"What are you doing here?" Selia kept her voice low as they pulled apart. Her eyes widened as she took in Anjy's left eye, purple and swollen shut, and her right one, blackened. Her nose was twice its normal size, dried blood caked at the nostrils.

"Who did this?" Selia gripped the basket so hard the wicker dug into her fist.

Anjy dropped her gaze. "My . . . husband."

Something sour squirmed in the pit of Selia's stomach. It had only been a few weeks. Anjy was already married? "What did your grandfather say, when he saw?"

"That I had it comin'," Anjy said. "That runnin' from sin wasn't enough, so it had to be beat from me."

"Creator," Bil murmured.

Selia felt a growl building in her throat. "Anyone know you're here?"

Anjy shook her head. "Snuck out the window, and it's nearing dusk. Don't think any in the market saw me, but Grandfather will come looking for me in the morning."

"And he'll know right where to look." Selia lifted the shawl around Anjy's shoulders up over her head. "But we can't stay here. Bil, be a dear and fetch Sallie Trigg. Ask her to come to the Speaker's house on the quick."

"Ay, Selia." Bil ran off as Selia made sure the path was clear and ushered Anjy along. The weather was chill enough that a head shawl was not so unusual, but they moved as quickly as possible past other folk and took a back path to her house.

"Selia, what . . . ?" Lory's question died on her lips as Selia pulled the shawl back and she took in Anjy's appearance. "Here, girl," Selia's mother pulled out a chair at the kitchen table, "let me get a cool cloth for your face." She looked to Selia. "Have you—"

"Sent Bil to fetch Sallie. Is Da . . . ?"

The front door opened, admitting Edwar, Sallie, and

Bil. Her father had no words as he watched Sallie tend to Anjy's face, but his balled fists said it all.

"Da, we can't let them—" Selia began.

Edwar silenced her with a raised hand. "We won't." He sat across from Anjy, his deep voice gentle and soothing. "Know it ent easy to talk about, Anjy, but I need to know who it was that hit you."

"My husband." Anjy bit her lip, trying to hold back tears. "Obi Watch."

The growl that had been building in Selia's throat broke free at last.

"Obi has more than fifty winters," Sallie said. "Man like that blessed with a wife less'n half his age should be thanking the Creator, not raising his hand."

"That's undersaid," Lory agreed.

"Nose is broke," Sallie said, "but there ent much for it but to rest and keep a cold compress on it till the swelling goes down. I'll work on a splint to see it heals straight." She ran a hand along Anjy's side, and the girl winced. Sallie looked at Bil. "Run along home now, Bil. Turn your back, Edwar."

Edwar dropped the bar across the door after Bil left, facing the kitchen window with his arms crossed and back turned. Sallie undid the fastenings and lowered Anjy's dress, revealing bruises—some dark and fresh, others yellowed and half healed.

"Night," Lory whispered.

"Nothin' else broken," Sallie said when her examination was finished. "Best let the girl rest."

"She can sleep in my bed," Selia blurted. When her parents turned, she dropped her eyes. "I'll sleep in the common."

Edwar nodded. The sun was setting as Sallie hurried

off home. Lory helped Anjy get cleaned up and into a nightdress, bringing her supper in bed. The rest of them ate in silence. Edwar's face was dark, and Selia and her mother knew better than to press him when he had that look.

Selia tossed and turned on the common-room floor after the lamps were turned down, waiting until her father's snores could be heard from the bedroom. Then she got up and slipped quietly into Anjy's room.

"Starting to think you weren't coming," Anjy said in the darkness.

"Caused enough trouble in that bed," Selia said. "Ent looking to make it worse."

"How's that?" Anjy asked. "You didn't make me marry a fat old man who hits me. You didn't tell Raddock Fisher he had a claim to your hand just because he's got a rich da. You didn't force Deardra to be a square girl against her will."

She reached out, fingers grasping in the darkness until she found Selia's hand. "What Selia Square did was run into the naked night and save me from corelings." She squeezed tight. "And make me feel like I wasn't alone."

Selia laid her free hand over the one Anjy held. "You ent. My da will fix this."

"Won't," Anjy said. "Grandfather ent one to let a thing go. Bring men with him come morning. Kick in the door and take me."

"Won't let them," Selia promised. "Figure a way out of this, sure as the sun rises."

"Already got it figured," Anjy said. "Going to the Free Cities."

Selia was glad of the darkness, hiding her gape. "Can't be serious."

"Didn't come today by accident," Anjy said. "Messenger's caravan just left, but they've got carts to haul. We cut across the Brook, we can get ahead of them up the road, too far to turn back before night. They'll camp on the way to Sunny Pasture, and we can hide in the carts."

It was a mad plan, but Selia barely registered it, her thoughts locking onto a single word. "We?"

"Go alone if I have to. Ent two thousand souls in the Brook. Hundred times as many in the Free Cities, the Jongleur's tales are true. Got to be square girls there." Anjy squeezed her hand again. "But I don't want any of them, there's a chance Selia Square wants me."

Selia choked. Only in her dreams had she heard such words. "Don't need to run to the ends of the world to be together, Anjy. Said it yourself. We didn't do any wrong. Why should we leave while they get to stay?"

"So no one else gets hurt over this," Anjy said.

"And if it's us that get hurt?" Selia asked. "What if we can't find the caravan before the sun sets? Corelings won't care who's wrong and who's right."

"Your da was a Messenger," Anjy said. "He still have his portable ward circle?"

"Ay," Selia said. "Gonna rob my da, on top of taking his daughter?"

Anjy pulled her hand back, and it was like she took a part of Selia with it. "Ent taking you, Selia. Ent Obi Watch or Raddock Fisher. Don't own you and you don't own me. Want you to come, but it's your choice."

There was a silence, and then whispered words in the darkness, almost too quiet to hear. "Love you, Selia Square."

Selia felt her chest constrict, and blew out a shuddering breath. She groped in the darkness, finding Anjy's hand and gripping tight. "Love you, Anjy Watch. Run with you.

Far as we need. Just askin' you to wait. Give my da time to sort things."

"Ent gonna have another chance, Selia," Anjy said. "Grandfather drags me back to Southwatch, don't think I'll get away so easy again."

"Da's Town Speaker," Selia said. "He can call a meeting. Sallie Trigg's a witness, and Bil Square. Town council can't ignore it. Whatever the Canon says about square girls, it's worse on men who raise hands to women."

"Won't matter," Anjy said, but she did not pull away again.

"Just give it a chance," Selia begged. "For me. For us."

Anjy was silent, but she tugged on Selia's hand, pulling her close. Selia followed the sound of her breathing, careful of her broken nose as she laid a gentle kiss on Anjy's lips.

6

Edwar was already out of the house when Selia woke. Lory had breakfast on and gave her a tray to take to Anjy.

"Speaker!" A voice boomed in the front yard. "Come for my granddaughter! Know you've got her!"

Selia stole a look from the window, careful not to be seen. Jeorje Watch was standing before a crowd of spear-wielding Watchmen. Night. How had he gotten here so quickly? Southwatch was miles away.

"Get away from the window," Lory said. Selia turned to see her mother pulling the spear off the mantelpiece. "Bar the door behind me, girl. Bar all the doors." Lory exited onto the porch, pulling the door shut behind her.

Selia did as she was told, barring the door, though she doubted it would do much good. Men willing to force their way past her mother wouldn't be hindered by a couple inches of wood.

She glanced at the rear entrance, then at the door to Anjy's room. Did Jeorje have men watching the back? If not, perhaps there was still time . . .

"Lot of men, to fetch one beat-up young woman!" Lory cried.

Selia put her back to the wall beside the window, looking out at an angle. It was a ludicrous sight—the town schoolmam holding off a crowd of armed Watchmen with her husband's old Messenger spear—but the determined look on Lory's face made Selia wonder if she just might do it.

"Ent your business, Lory Square!" Jeorje shouted back. "Stand aside!"

"Whole town's business when a man raises his hand to his wife," Lory replied. "Girl came to the Speaker's house for succor, and we've granted it."

Jeorje spread his hands, approaching. "We're her family, not corelings, and we both know that's not why Anjy chose your house."

Lory lifted the spear. "That's far enough, Jeorje."

Jeorje smiled, continuing to step forward. "Give me my granddaughter, and we'll be off your property and on our way. You can't stop us."

"Perhaps not, but we can!" Edwar's voice carried across the yard. Selia dared to step in front of the window, breathing a sigh of relief as she saw her father approaching with what looked like half the men in town. Big burly Cutters with axe mattocks across their shoulders, Baleses and Pastures with picks and hoes, Boggins with cooper's hammers, and Squares with an assortment of tools and hunting spears.

They outnumbered the Watches, but not by so much

that Jeorje couldn't cause trouble. He turned to face Edwar, leaving Lory forgotten at his back. He opened his mouth, but before he could speak, Edwar cut him off.

"Obi Watch!" Edwar pointed to a middle-aged man, thick about the middle, with a round face and a beard shot through with gray. "You are accused of beating your wife! How do you plead?"

Obi's jaw dropped and his eyes widened. "Don't owe you explanations about what goes on in my home!"

"Oh, but you think you've a right to break into mine?" Edwar shot back.

"You've no proof I've done anything!" Obi sputtered.

"We have Anjy as witness," Edwar said.

"Her word against mine." Obi's voice was gaining confidence. "No proof. Girl fell down the steps."

"You live in a ranch," Edwar shot back. "Sallie Trigg examined her. Willing to bet, we measure your fist, it will fit her bruises."

Obi scowled, balling a fist and shaking it at Edwar. "Want my fist, Square, that can be arranged."

Edwar didn't hesitate, stepping up until the two men were nose to nose. "Easy to hit a girl half your size. Got the stones to try it on me?" He smiled, sticking out his chin and closing his eyes. "Even let you throw the first punch. Swear by the sun I'll throw the last."

"Enough." Jeorje was on the defensive now, but seemed no less dangerous for it. He pulled back Obi, who looked much relieved. "Ent a trial, Speaker. Can't expect—"

"Ay, you're right," Edwar cut him off again. "Calling the town council to meet on the matter tomorrow. You and Obi can discuss his plea then."

Jeorje's calm veneer began to crack, a hint of snarl on his face. "Doesn't settle the matter of my granddaughter."

Edwar crossed his arms. "No, it doesn't. But unless

you want to try and cross my wards to take her, we'll settle this first."

"Not with the girl staying in your house of sin," Jeorje said. "It may be her leading your daughter astray, or the other way around, but I won't have it."

There was some mumbling among the townsfolk on Edwar's side at the words, and Jeorje smiled, sensing his advantage. "Haven't told them the whole story, have you, Speaker?"

"She can stay with me," Sallie Trigg cut in, before Edwar could reply. "I've sickbeds, and need to tend her nose in any event. You can post guards if you like, though I hope it ent necessary."

Jeorje looked like he had just sucked a lemon dry, but he nodded. "Agreed. But she's to be moved now, and I'll see her with my own eyes."

Selia stood protectively in front of Anjy's door as Sallie and the men came into the house to take her. The Watches remained outside save for Jeorje, whose eyes bored into Selia. "Stand aside, girl."

Selia bunched a fist, but Edwar stepped between them and laid a hand on her shoulder. "Trust me. Ent gonna let anything happen to her. We'll make this right."

Selia let out a breath, allowing her father to pull her aside, but when he tried the latch, the door was barred.

"Anjy!" He knocked loudly on the door. "It's Edwar. Ent no one going to hurt you, girl. Just taking you to the Triggs' to be looked after while the council sorts this out."

There was no reply, and Edwar knocked again. "Ent the time for games! You're under my roof. This door ent open at the count of ten, I'll break it down!"

"Da—" Selia began, but Edwar cut her off with a raised hand, beginning to count.

Still there was no response. Edwar pounded one last time. "Once Sallie says you're better, you'll be staying in town till you work off the cost of a new door!" Then he gave the door a kick.

The heavy wood shuddered but did not break. Banded with iron and cut with polished wards, it was meant to be a last defense if corelings made it into the house.

Edwar did not relent. When her father set himself to a task, Selia knew there was nothing to do but stand aside and let him see it done. Again and again he kicked and threw his shoulder against the door. Jeorje joined him, and together they broke the bar at last, tumbling into the room atop the splintering door.

But the bed was empty, window open, curtains wafting softly in the breeze.

Anjy was gone.

"Where is she?!" Jeorje grabbed Selia's arm. She swung a fist at him, but he swatted it aside, tightening his painful grip.

Jeorje lost his wide-brimmed hat as Edwar's right cross slammed his head into a support beam, but he kept his feet. He shook away the effects of the blow and came at Edwar with his guard in place, but whatever passed for fisticuffs in Southwatch was no match for a Milnese Messenger's training. Edwar caught Jeorje's blows on his arms and laid him on his back with an uppercut that nearly made the Southwatch Speaker bite off his tongue.

"Lay hands on my daughter again, you'll be spending months on one of Sallie Trigg's sickbeds," Edwar warned.

Jeorje growled, but he spread his hands as he got to his

feet. "Ay, Speaker. You're her father. You handle it. But if my granddaughter isn't in safe succor by nightfall, we'll be holding your family to account."

Edwar turned to Selia. "Any idea where she might have gone?"

"Where can she go," Selia said, "when her husband beats her with her grandfather cheering him on? When the Town Speaker's house ent safe succor?"

"Ent an answer, girl," Jeorje said.

Selia screwed her face into a look of vapid anxiety, squeezing out tears that came surprisingly easily. She waited as long as she dared, giving Anjy time to run before blurting out an answer they were apt to believe. "Said last night, we didn't take her, she'd go to the Holy House. Ask Tender Stewert for succor."

Jeorje grunted and turned, heading for the door. Edwar and the others quickly followed.

"You all right?" Lory put a hand on her shoulder. "Let me make you a cup of tea and we can—"

Selia pulled away. "Just want to be alone."

Lory pursed her lips, but she nodded, putting the spear back on the mantel. "All right. Be in the kitchen, you change your mind."

The moment she left, Selia took the spear and headed to the stable.

*

Selia walked the horse quietly out the back way, then swung into a saddle and kicked off once she was far enough from the house. Her own shield lost, she had taken her father's, as well as his portable ward circle and some hasty supplies from the cold room.

She rode north, then cut overland, trying to guess what

path a young woman on foot, trying to avoid being seen, might take. By midmorning she realized she'd gone farther than Anjy could have run and doubled back, trying another route. That, too, was a failure. Afternoon came, bringing with it a growing sense of dread as the sun began its slow descent. Should she press on to the road and try to find the Messenger caravan, or double back a second time?

There were a hundred ways Anjy could have taken, including several not suited to a rider on horseback. Selia pressed on instead, finding the road to Sunny Pasture and the Messenger caravan soon after.

"Selia!" Jahn cried as she rode up to them. "What in the dark of night are you doing all the way out here?"

"Looking for Anjy Watch." Selia swung down from her saddle, thighs aching. "Husband beat her, and she ran off. Said she was looking for you, hoping to steal away to the Free Cities."

"Corespawn it." Jahn spat on the ground. "Ent seen her."

Selia glanced at the sun, dangerously low. "Said she might hide in your carts."

Jahn's men searched the caravan, but there was no sign of Anjy. Selia put a foot back in her stirrup. "Need to find her."

Jahn put a hand on her shoulder. "Ent letting you . . ." the words died on his lips as Selia turned her glare his way, ". . . go alone."

Selia kissed his cheek. "Knew I could count on you, Uncle Jahn."

Jahn sent men back the way they'd come while he and Selia rode up ahead, calling Anjy's name and scanning the roadside for paths in the scrub.

"Getting dark," Jahn said at last. "We should head back."

"Not without Anjy," Selia said.

"Maybe the others found her," Jahn suggested.

"They'd have sounded their horns," Selia said.

Jahn did not argue. "Won't help her by getting cored, Selia."

"Go back if you want," Selia said. "Got Da's portable circle. I'll be all right."

Jahn barked a laugh. "You're on tampweed, you think I'll leave Edwar's daughter alone in the dark, circle or no."

They searched a little longer, Selia screaming Anjy's name until her throat was hoarse, all to no avail. At last, Jahn gripped her horse's reins. "We don't put our circles down now, we're no good to anyone. If she comes running down the road at rising, at least we can offer succor."

Selia nodded, tightening her jaw to stay tears as she hobbled her horse and followed the lessons her father had drilled into her for laying the circle.

Jahn built a fire, offering her a drink from his canteen and some dried meat. "Ent much, but you look like you haven't had anything all day."

Selia took the canteen, drinking greedily as the sun slipped below the horizon and the rising began.

At first there was no sign of corelings. Demons tended to cluster near human habitations, and here, on the road between towns, Selia and Jahn were some distance from even the most isolated farms. It wasn't until she heard the shriek of a wind demon that Selia knew the corelings had come.

There were other shrieks, corelings answering the windie's call, or in pursuit of prey.

But then, over the sounds of demons, came a cry much more familiar.

"Selia . . . !" Jahn warned, but she ignored him, leaping to her feet and snatching up her father's spear and shield. He scrambled to grab her ankle, but missed and fell face-first on the ground as Selia left the circle, running quietly up the road.

❦

Selia turned from the road, trusting her ears as much as her eyes, barely able to spot the opening in the scrub in the moonlight. Every crunch of her feet filled her with dread. She might not be able to see in darkness, but the corelings could, and their senses were far stronger than hers. If they found her before she reached Anjy, she didn't think much of her chances.

Idiot girl, she thought. *Ent got much chance you do find her, either.*

Still she ran on, following Anjy's cries and the shrieks of corelings. The sounds were . . . frustrated, and when Selia caught a flash of magic ahead, she slowed, daring to hope.

A wood demon was circling a tree, swiping at a forbidding in the form of painted wardplates laid around the trunk. Light flared each time the coreling struck, the wards glowing with residual power as it faded. Selia could see the wards were spread thin. They might be enough to hold one demon back, but . . .

A low growl heralded the approach of a field demon, padding slowly around the scene, unnoticed by Anjy and the wood demon alike. Field demons were fast on open ground, but it stalked carefully amid the trees, watching the flare of wards, noting the gaps in their overlapping protection.

Selia looked up, seeing Anjy cowering in the boughs.

She was trying to keep quiet, but every time the woodie slammed one of its branchlike arms against the forbidding, she let out a cry as if she herself had been struck.

Human cries are a Jongleur's song to demons, Edwar taught. *They'll kill anything they can find, but it's humans they hunger for.*

If Anjy didn't quiet soon, it was only a matter of time before more were drawn to the commotion.

The wood demon struck again, claws whining as they skittered across the magic. They caught fast on a seam where the plates didn't quite overlap and, in the flare of wardlight, a thin gap appeared.

It was all the field demon needed. It tamped down and pounced, closing the distance in two quick bounds. Its front legs and head made it through the opening, but the gap was too narrow to admit the demon's shoulders and the coreling was caught fast.

But not for long. Its talons hooked into the bark of the tree, gouging deep furrows and pulling itself through, inch by inch. Above, Anjy screamed, no doubt signaling their position to every Wanderer in the area.

Selia knew she could wait no longer. She laid her course, then ducked her head and shoulders behind the rounded shield, charging in at the demons.

Alone, Selia didn't have the strength and weight to dislodge the field demon, but when she smashed into its flank, the wards around her father's shield blazed to life, tearing the demon's talons from the tree and knocking the coreling into the wood demon still clawing at the forbidding beside it. They were knocked sprawling and Selia stepped across the barrier to stand protectively in front of the tree, spear and shield at the ready.

"Selia!" Anjy cried. "Creator be praised! What are you doing here?"

"Looking for you, woodbrain," Selia growled. "Had me running all over the Brook trying to find you. Now shut it. You're drawing more of them."

Anjy slipped down from the branches to stand behind Selia, a heavy branch in her hands. "I'm sorry. You shouldn't have come."

Selia spared a glance from the regrouping demons to look back at her. "Told you I'd follow you. Far as we need."

Anjy sobbed, kissing her cheek as Selia turned back to face the demons. With her foot, she nudged one of the wardplates in front of her. As expected, the field demon came in at the exact same spot, this time running face-first into a wall of magic. Selia punctuated this with a bash from her shield, knocking it back again.

"Can't keep this up all night," she said.

"What else can we do?" Anjy asked.

"Got Messenger circles less than half a mile down the road," Selia said. "We get the chance, we run. Quick and quiet as can be."

Anjy nodded, but the chance seemed increasingly unlikely as a second wood demon appeared. The three demons began circling the tree, smashing and clawing at the wards, sensing weakness just beyond their primitive brains' ability to puzzle out. They could only search by sight and feel, dragging talons across the forbidding and looking for patches of dark amid the flaring wardlight.

One of the wood demons stuck a limb into a gap, stubbornly swiping and clawing even as Selia stepped to the side and bashed at the limb with her shield. Woodies were larger and heavier than fieldies, and even the wards of her father's great shield could not dislodge it.

Anjy struck the arm with her branch until the flailing claws caught hold of it, flinging her hard against the trunk of the tree. She was smart enough to let go, falling to hands and knees right in front of the charging field demon. Wardlight rose to thwart the attack, but there was a gap and the demon stuck its snout through, rows of razor-sharp teeth snapping the air and spattering her with saliva.

Selia stepped around the tree to come at them from the other side as the field demon scrunched and wriggled, working a limb through the gap to swipe at Anjy, who put her back to the tree. The wood demon appeared stuck, unable to penetrate farther or withdraw. It clawed at the tree, shaking free nuts, leaves, and dead branches that pattered down like rain.

The field demon clawed at the thick roots, pulling itself forward. It snapped at Selia and she thrust her spear hard down its throat, praying its armor was weaker on the inside.

It seemed she was right. The demon choked and convulsed, scrabbling desperately backward. Its jaws snapped shut, breaking the thick goldwood spear shaft like kindling. Selia slammed the demon with her shield for good measure, knocking it from the gap. The demon rolled in the scrub, hacking and growling, then seemed to think better of the fight and fled, the spearhead still in its belly.

Selia wanted to cheer, but the small victory made little difference. The trapped wood demon was tearing through the tree like a pair of cutters, ripping off large pieces of trunk. It was only a matter of time before the growing debris obscured Anjy's warding, or the tree itself collapsed, taking the forbidding with it.

The second wood demon stalked in, but then something struck it on the back with the sound of breaking glass. The demon looked over its shoulder in confusion, then shrieked as fires blazed all over its body.

"Selia! Run!" Jahn had a short spear slung over his shoulder and carried a blazing torch in his shield hand. He threw a glass vial that shattered on impact with the demon still stuck in the forbidding, spattering it with fluid. He took the torch in his spear hand and set it alight.

Selia didn't hesitate, dropping her broken spear shaft and grabbing Anjy's hand. She hauled her along as they fled back to the road.

Their eyes, accustomed to the blaze of wardlight, took time to adjust to the darkness of the woods, even with the glow of fire at their backs. They stumbled on, Selia leading with her shield to keep them from running into anything solid.

A moment later Jahn caught up to them, torch still in hand to light their way. "Just lamp oil. Won't stop them for long. They'll roll on the ground till it's out, then come after us twice as mad."

The three of them ran as fast as they could, lurching through the brush. Selia slipped and banged her knee on a root, biting back the pain as she bounced right back to her feet and kept running. Thornbushes caught at Anjy's skirts, and Jahn gave no thought to her modesty, tearing cloth until she was free.

They made the road and put on speed until the campfire, horses, and warded circles were in sight.

But the camp had drawn Wanderers. Half a dozen demons stood between them and succor.

❦

Field demons raced their way, and Jahn put his shield out at an angle. "Wedge!"

Selia understood, angling her shield to mirror his,

forming a point as they charged. Wards flashed and the demons were deflected, stumbling to keep their feet. A flame demon spat at them, but the sticky firespit found no purchase on the wards, winking out in midair. Jahn kicked the demon aside and they put on a burst of speed.

The circles were close when one of the field demons caught up with them from behind, teeth closing on the trailing cloth of Anjy's torn skirts. Her hand yanked from Selia's grasp as she fell.

"Run on!" Jahn turned to face the demons, dropping his torch to pull the spear from its harness on his back.

The Messenger was clad in warded armor, better prepared to face the demons, but Selia hadn't come all this way to abandon her friend. She tackled the demon while it was still pulling on the cloth of Anjy's skirt. Selia took a handful of the thick black cloth and wrapped it around the demon's head, tangling its jaws as Anjy tried to wriggle free of the skirt.

Anjy managed to get clear, clad only in her bloomers. She screamed as the demon's blindly scrabbling claws raked her thigh, drawing dark lines of blood in the dim light.

Jahn kicked the demon onto its back, thrusting his spear hard into its unarmored belly. The point penetrated, but not deeply. Still, the demon gave a muffled cry beneath the cloth, wriggling desperately.

Jahn threw his shield on the ground, face-up. "Stand on the shields!"

Messenger shields were wide and round, with concentric circles of wards starting at the outer rim. They were designed, in a moment of last resort, to be miniature circles of protection, just large enough for a single person to stand upon.

"What about you?" Selia cried.

"I have my armor!" Jahn pointed to her shield. "Selia Square, for once in your corespawned life, do as you're told!"

The demons were circling, and Selia knew he was right. She threw down her own shield, helping Anjy shakily to her feet and onto the shield.

"I don't think I can stand."

"You have to!" Selia had just enough time to leap onto Jahn's shield as a field demon pounced. She had to gather her skirt, but the wards held, knocking the demon back.

Jahn was less fortunate. The flame demon leapt at him and the wards on his armor knocked it away, but the rebound sent him stumbling. A field demon sensed his imbalance and used the rebound to knock him from his feet.

They were all around him now, swiping, biting, and spitting. His armor held, but the weight of the metal, the exhaustion from their desperate flight, and the continued blows from the corelings were overwhelming. He struggled to rise.

"Get back to the circles!" Selia shouted to him.

Too harried to argue, Jahn began a slow crawl back to the camp. Inch by inch he made his way, sometimes managing a staggering step or two before being brought back down. Dirt crusted the wards etched on his armor now, and demon talons began to gouge and scratch the metal. One raking claw slipped from a plate into the unwarded metal links at the back of his knee, and Jahn screamed.

Still he crawled, drawing attention from Selia and Anjy as he drew closer and closer to the camp. At last he reached the circles and rolled across to safety.

The corelings smashed at the barrier for a time, then

lost interest, turning back to more vulnerable prey. Selia wrapped her skirt tight with a fold and tuck to hold it close inside the shield's circle while leaving her hands free.

She looked at Anjy, bare-legged, and saw the young woman shaking. Blood ran down her wounded thigh, pooling at her feet and running over the wards, weakening the protection.

The demons smelled blood and fear in the air, ignoring Selia and Jahn to focus on Anjy. They paced around her shield, hissing and growling at one another, each seeking to be the first to sink its teeth into Anjy when she inevitably collapsed.

"Selia!" Jahn hissed from the protection of one of the circles as Selia slowly squatted down, stepping off the shield and slipping it back onto her arm.

Anjy's leg buckled, and the young woman stumbled, falling off the shield. A flame demon leapt at her as Selia charged in. She met the demon head-on with a shield bash that knocked it across the road in a flash of magic.

She caught Anjy with her free arm, supporting her as she waved her shield at the other demons.

"Leave me!" Anjy cried.

"Going to be all right," Selia said with assurance she didn't feel. "We'll walk to the circles, nice and slow. Pick up your shield."

A field demon pounced as Anjy reached for the bloody shield, but it was knocked aside in a flare of light.

Selia looked back to see Jahn throw a warded stone, scattering a trio of demons. "Forget the shield! Go now!"

"Come on," Selia said, half supporting, half dragging Anjy toward the circles. She was still losing blood, eyelids heavy and movements clumsy.

Another field demon charged Anjy, slavering for her bloody bare thigh. Jahn missed his throw, but Selia thrust her shield in its path, then threw her shoulder into it, knocking the demon sprawling.

Still they moved, the circles just a few feet away.

But then there was a shriek and a flap of wings. Suddenly a wind demon was right next to her, so close Selia could smell its horrid stench and feel its leathern skin as it dug its talons into Anjy's body. Anjy tried to cry, but it came out as a gout of blood.

Selia was buffeted as the demon flapped its wings again, taking off as quickly as it had appeared. Without thinking, Selia swung her shield as she was knocked back, the wind wards along its edge striking the joint where the thin bones of the demon's wing met the shoulder.

There was a crack, and the wing collapsed. The demon had been rising swiftly into the air, and it came crashing down atop Anjy, the impact pushing the claws buried in her back out through her front.

"Anjy!" Selia shrieked, but before she could regain her feet, the other demons struck, tearing into the young woman and rending her apart. Selia screamed, raising her shield to charge into them.

"Selia, corespawn it!" Jahn had come limping from the circle to grab her arm. "She's dead! We'll be, too, if we don't get back to the circle right ripping now!"

Selia sobbed, but she stumbled along with him until they stepped over the circle. She fell to her knees, seeing her dress soaked in Anjy's blood.

And she wailed.

🜨

What they found the next day was barely recognizable as human, just bones and blood and bits of clothing. Enough to fill a small box for a symbolic funeral pyre, but nothing compared to the woman Anjy had been. The woman she might have become, given the chance.

"Take me with you," Selia told Jahn. "Let me come to the Free Cities, and corespawn Tibbet's Brook."

"Like night I will. Can't just run away from your problems, Selia." Jahn nodded to the box. "They'll catch up to you every time."

It was late in the day when the caravan rode back into Town Square. She expected her father to shout, to rage that she had lied, but he only swept her into his arms and wept.

The town council was less forgiving. Tender Stewert, the Triggs, and the Speakers from every borough listened as Jeorje laid bare her and Anjy's love like some kind of crime. Selia sat through it at her father's side, eyes down, too tired to fight anymore. What did it matter, now that there was no one to fight for?

"Selia Square's sinful ways are a burden on this town," Jeorje said. "My granddaughter is dead, murdered much as if this girl had done it with her own hands. I demand she be held to account."

"Lies." Edwar bashed a fist against the table. "Selia didn't banish Anjy to Town Square. Selia didn't force her to marry an old man who raised his hand to her. Selia didn't come to drag her back to that corespawned house when she fled in terror. If any are to blame for this, Jeorje Watch, it's you and Obi. Stake yourselves in the square, if you want justice."

Jeorje bared his teeth, but he and Edwar were only two voices on a council of many.

"Jeorje's got a point, Edwar," Isak said. "If not for Selia, Deardra—"

"Demonshit," Edwar cut him off. "Don't blame your

daughter's choices on Selia. She's grown, and knew she was kissing the woman her brother shined on. Did my daughter cast some magic spell out of a Jongleur's tale on her?"

"No," Isak said. "But if you had taken a firmer hand with her . . ."

"Then what?" Edwar demanded. "I could have driven my own child into the naked night like Jeorje did with his granddaughter?"

"Maybe," Angos Marsh said. "Or maybe knocked enough sense into her to come to you when the Watch girl ran off."

"She came to me." Jahn, still in his armor, scraped and gouged from battle, cut an impressive figure none could ignore. "Selia Square may be willful, but in the naked night she risked her life again and again for her friend. If that's a sinner, I never understood a single Seventhday sermon."

"Might be you didn't," Jeorje said.

Jahn crossed his arms. "And might be the Duke needs his salt more than he needs trade with Southwatch."

"Enough," Edwar said. "On the matter of Obi Watch, punishment for raising your hand to a woman is ten lashes. What does the council say?"

Nine hands rose, Jeorje alone abstaining. He scowled, but nodded. "I'll administer them personally." Obi turned to look at him wide-eyed, but Jeorje met his look, daring the man to argue, and Obi wisely kept silent. "Now, on the matter of Selia Square, accused of murder—"

"No one but you is accusing her of murder, Watch," Angos Marsh sneered. "Girl ent an innocent, whatever the Messenger says, but I ent going to be party to putting some girl out in the night to rub your ego."

Jeorje's fists clenched, eyes scanning the rest of the

room. Isak Fisher nodded to him. "Marsh has a point. Selia ent a murderer, but she needs punishment."

"Nonsense," Sallie Trigg said. "Selia ent done anything but right by Anjy Watch."

"Ay," Harve Trigg agreed.

"And you, Tender?" Edwar asked.

Stewert wrung his hands, looking from Edwar to Jahn to Jeorje. At last he sighed. "If Selia can abandon her . . . ways, the Creator can forgive. But not without punishment for bringing false witness, naming the Creator's holy succor to lead you astray in your search."

Selia looked up at that. "Would you have given it? Would you have protected her?"

Tender Stewert leveled her a disapproving stare. "We'll never know now, will we, child?"

"Ten lashes, same as Obi." Jeorje slammed his copy of the Canon down on the table.

"And what of you, Jeorje?" Edwar demanded. "Your part in this is no less than Obi's or Selia's. Will you accept ten lashes, as well?"

Selia could tell Edwar expected the Speaker for Southwatch to balk, but Jeorje smiled. "I will."

Edwar blinked, stunned.

"All in favor?" Jeorje asked, before Edwar could manage a reply.

The punishment was kept private, with only the council to bear witness. Edwar would let no other swing the lash, but he did not lighten his hand for his daughter.

It didn't matter. Selia felt nothing as the whip struck.

5

The Vote

334 AR

The Tibbet's Brook charter was an ancient document, dating nearly back to the Return, but it had kept the Brook in relative peace for all that time. It laid out the rules for voting, and required prospective Speakers to arrive at a vote unarmed and unarmored.

Selia reluctantly left her spear, shield, and armor behind, arriving in the same dress she'd worn on voting day for decades. It didn't fit as it once had. New muscles strained sleeves meant for thinner arms and chest; the waist hung loose around her slim stomach. Around her neck she wore a brookstone necklace carved with mind wards.

The entire town turned out. Squares, Boggins, Baleses, Pastures, Cutters, and more. They looked sadly at Selia, letting their eyes drift over Lesa as they nervously rolled the wooden balls Hog was handing out in their palms. Many had drawn mind wards on their foreheads. Others wore necklaces like Selia's, hats with warded bands, or embroidered headscarves.

The Fishers looked belligerent, glaring angrily at Selia and sneering at Lesa. Like the Watches, they were armed, and Selia wondered if things had truly fallen so far they might use them. There were more Marshes than Selia had ever seen in town—more than she had realized there were. They were mud-stained and dirty, faces grim, but many clutched frog spears in one hand and voting balls in the other.

The Watches looked triumphant. How long had they waited for this day? They worshipped Jeorje, and Selia held little hope for a single dissenting vote among them. Jeorje flouted the charter, leaning on his cane and wearing his heavy black coat, the lining sewn with plates of warded glass. He gave his customary hint of smile, daring her to try to deprive the oldest man in the Brook of the walking stick he'd carried for fifty years.

When the crowd was fully gathered, Selia left Lesa and went up to the stage erected in the square, standing to the right with Meada, Coline, Brine, Harral, and Jeph. On the far side stood Jeorje, Raddock, Coran, and . . . Hog. Selia glared at him, but the Speaker for the Square only shrugged.

"Hog's taking two-to-one odds under the counter on Jeorje taking the gavel," Brine said. "Ent such a fool as to be seen voting on the losing side."

"He'll feel the fool when Jeorje hauls off half his inventory as sinful," Harral said.

"I know Hog," Meada said. "He's already hidden his ale stores someplace safe to sell after Jeorje starts prohibition."

"Always profit in sufferin'," Jeph agreed.

"Someone else run," Selia said. "Brook's more important than my pride."

"You can't mean that!" Meada was aghast.

"Can and do," Selia said. "Jeph?"

Jeph Bales' jaw dropped. "Me?"

"Your fault we're in this mess," Selia said. "Folk know the Messenger is your son, now. They seen the strength of your wards. Might be you can win this."

Jeph shook his head. "Don't know that, Selia. Got my own share of scandals, and the Fishers and Marshes are going to vote with the Watches no matter what. Besides, ent qualified to lead the militia tonight."

Selia looked at Brine. "Ay, don't look at me. Never wanted that job."

"Folk know I'll just defer to you anyway," Meada said before Selia could call on her. Harral and Coline stepped back. Tender and Herb Gatherer commanded respect in town, but neither were eager to lead in times of trouble.

"Just look weaker, you bow out," Jeph said. "Town ent gonna abandon you, Selia. Got to trust in that."

The Speaker for Southwatch stepped out to center stage, thumping his cane until the crowd fell silent. "Sunlight's wastin', so we'll get right to it. New moon comes again tonight, and we all remember what happened last month, when everything was nearly lost due to the poor leadership of Speaker Selia."

"Ay, that's a rippin' lie!" Brine shouted. "Whole Brook would have been overrun, not for Selia!"

"Tell that to my kin, with our borough burned to the ground while you were lost in the woods!" Raddock shouted back.

"Had a month to debate," Raddock went on. "Everyone knows why we're here. I call for a vote of no faith in Speaker Selia. She's been showin' poor judgment for fifty years, and now, in our darkest hour, we need new leadership."

It wasn't the first time something like this had happened. Raddock had wrested the Speaker's gavel from her more than once over the years. The drought of 305 AR. The time demons burned the fields in 321. Always, the gavel reverted to her on the next vote, after Raddock made things worse. But this time, Selia knew it was different.

"I nominate Jeorje Watch as Town Speaker!"

Everyone knew it was coming, but it was a blow all the same. There were excited whispers throughout the crowd. Always before, the vote for Town Speaker had been split three ways: Raddock, Jeorje, and Selia. There had been competition between Raddock and Selia before, but the Southwatch Speaker had never come close to taking the gavel.

Brine stepped forward next. "I nominate Selia Square!"

Selia rubbed her temple, trying to massage away the tension.

A long silence followed, and at last Jeorje thumped his cane and Hog put two sealed barrels beneath the curtain frame at center stage. One was marked with a square, the other a cane. He tilted the barrels to show the Speakers they were empty, then hammered the slotted tops on and drew the curtain closed to keep the ballot secret.

Selia took a deep breath. As Town Speaker, the first vote was hers. She walked behind the curtain and put her ball in the square barrel.

Jeorje came next, a cruel smile on his face as he stepped from the curtain.

Raddock, Jeph, and the other Speakers voted in turn. Coline stood behind the curtain a long time. Regardless of her vote, the hesitation was telling.

The Speakers withdrew as folk lined up, coming up one side of the stage to cast their votes and going down the other. There were over a thousand voters, and not all were quick about it. More than one had tears in their eyes as they left the curtain. Others stood undecided a long time, as Coline had.

Tensions grew as the sun climbed into the sky and dipped back down. The last vote was cast, and they set to counting, with the Speakers verifying every vote.

"Five hundred thirty-seven for Jeorje Watch," Hog called at last. "For Selia Square, five hundred forty-two."

Selia's eyebrows raised. Was it possible?

The crowd, taut as a reeling fishing line, burst into chatter at that, until Jeorje banged his cane against the boards. "One thousand fifty-nine voters, I counted, yet we have one thousand seventy-nine votes?"

"Cheat!" Raddock roared.

And up came the spears.

&

The square erupted into a melee the likes of which Tibbet's Brook had never seen. Old grudges, held in check for years by civilized life, burst their stitches as that façade fell away.

Stam Tailor was tackled by Maddy's father and brothers. Garric Fisher broke a spear across the back of Lucik's head. When Meada ran to him, Nomi Fisher leapt on her shoulders, bearing her down and clawing at her. Jeph jumped off the stage to assist her, but Mack Pasture caught him by the shoulder and punched him in the face.

The incidents were not isolated—hundreds of similar dramas reaching their climax as neighbor fought neighbor. Some had weapons; others used whatever was to hand, or bare knuckles. Fishers, tired of being pushed around. Marshes, tired of the scorn of the other boroughs.

"Stop this! There was no cheat!" Selia screamed over the din, but if anyone noticed, they gave no sign.

"Numbers don't lie, Selia," Jeorje said. "Have you done this every year? How else could a sinner and murderer have Spoken for the town so long?"

He lifted his cane and came for her, and Selia, without weapons or armor, was ill prepared to fight. She gave ground as he advanced. Were the numbers wrong? Who knew how many had come from the Marsh? From Southwatch? All they had was Jeorje's word. Had this been his plan all along?

Brine stepped in front of her. Close to seven feet tall and built like a goldwood tree, he towered over Jeorje, handling the heavy axe mattock in his hands like a hatchet. "Want to touch the Speaker, need to go through me."

Jeorje smiled, then came in fast. Brine grabbed at him with his free hand, unwilling to strike another man with his weapon even now. Jeorje took full advantage, sliding around the off-handed swipe to crack the head of his cane against the back of Brine's knee. Broadshoulders roared as the leg bucked and he stumbled. It was all the opening Jeorje needed for a second strike, breaking Brine's jaw.

"Get Coline out of here," Selia told Harral. "Take anyone you can to the Holy House and lock the doors."

Brine dropped to the stage, stunned. Jeorje raised his cane for a finishing blow, but Selia leapt and tackled him. Raddock charged her, but she rolled to her feet and met him head-on, locking his arm and neck in a clinch that left his midsection unprotected as her knee came up hard, blowing the breath from him. Before he could recover, she kneed him again. And a third time.

Jeorje had recovered his feet by then but Selia pivoted and threw Raddock's limp body into his path. The stage was narrow and, with no room to dodge, the two men went down in a tangle.

"Selia!" Lesa had been attacked by a pair of Watchmen. One lay moaning on the ground. The other was stumbling away, screaming as he cradled a broken arm. Heedless of her own safety, Lesa threw her spear. Selia caught it gratefully as Jeorje shoved Raddock away and got to his feet, murder in his eyes.

"Security!" Hog called. His fighters appeared, armed and armored, a disciplined group amid the chaos. Selia let out a breath.

"Protect the store!" Hog cried.

"Corespawn you, Rusco Hog!" Selia cried, but it was herself she was angry with for ever trusting the man to act in anyone's interests but his own.

Indeed, more folk in the Brook held grudges against Hog than anyone. Already looters were running out of the store with armfuls of goods. Catrin chased a group out with a rolling pin, but there was blood in her hair. There was no sign of Dasy, Hog's other daughter.

Smaller shops around the square were no safer, folk taking what they could as the owners desperately tried to protect their goods or struggled with Jeorje's men.

The Cutters did what they could to restore order, but they were brawlers more than disciplined fighters. Selia's militia was organized, but no more so than the Watchmen, who came at them, spears leading.

"Stop this!" Selia screamed at Jeorje as he stalked toward her. "The sun is setting!"

But Jeorje only smiled, and then she knew.

⚶

Selia quit trying to reason, to keep the violence boiling in her breast in check. The town, her town, was in danger, and Jeorje was in her way. The demon had done something while it was in his mind. Something that carried into the day.

She raised her spear and charged.

Jeorje flicked his cane, unsheathing the spear tip at the end as he planted his feet to meet her. Selia held her spear in two hands, whipping it at him like a quarterstaff, coming at him from both sides.

But Jeorje was fast, the ancient man batting the blows aside with the head of his cane and then lifting it to thrust the tip right at her heart. Selia felt it tear through her blouse and cut into her breast as she twisted out of its path. She swung her spear shaft down to trip him, but Jeorje was wise to the move, hopping over the wood like a child skipping rope. Selia's nose flattened with a crunch as he turned a full circuit to put an elbow into her face.

Lights went off behind her eyes as a shock of pain lanced through her. Selia let the blow crumple her—only half a feint. Jeorje took the bait, raising his cane to drive the spearpoint into her back. As his guard dropped, Selia rolled over and punched hard between his legs.

Jeorje let out a hoarse cry but kept his feet. Selia hit him again and he stumbled back, clutching a hand protectively over his crotch. She knew she should press the attack, but her head was ringing and she took the chance to grab her spear and get back to her feet.

She glanced around to find Keven Marsh creeping up on her. He dropped his spear crosswise over her head and pulled tight, choking her even as Jeorje stalked back in.

Lesa vaulted onto the stage, kicking Keven in the knee. Selia elbowed him in the ribs as he stumbled, and he lost his grip. She stepped away, and Lesa, a Watch spear in her hands, put her back to Selia's.

Smoke was in the air, fire coming from Stam Tailor's shop and threatening to spread even as the shadows grew long. Some of the folk fled to succor, but others were caught up fighting and looting, caring for wounded, or lying unconscious like poor Brine. There were bodies, blood, and debris on the cobbles, hopelessly marring the greatward as the sun began to set.

"Quit holding back." Selia wasn't sure if she was speaking to Lesa or herself. The two of them moved as one, giving up their defensive position to strike.

Lesa was faster and more agile than Keven, landing blows more often, but Keven was bigger, stronger, and shrugged off much of what his armor failed to turn. Selia tried to make up for her lack of armor with speed and ferocity, but Jeorje had the advantage. He was unable to set up a killing thrust, but he battered Selia with lesser blows that began to accumulate. Her muscles burned from exertion, bones bruised and likely a few cracked.

She feigned greater weakness than she felt, and when Jeorje prepared to strike she put her spear into his wrist, causing him to drop his cane.

He wasn't taken completely unawares. Even as the cane fell away, Selia's spear was out of alignment and she could do nothing to stop his strong right hand from grabbing her by the throat. He kicked her feet from under her, slamming her down hard onto the stage.

"Selia!" Lesa screamed, but the moment of distraction cost her as Keven push-kicked her off the stage. She landed heavily on the cobbles and he leapt down atop her even as Jeorje began to squeeze. His left hand joined the other, blood running from his wrist, hot and slippery on Selia's chest. His face was twisted with hate, spittle running from clenched teeth.

Selia struggled, pulling at his arms, but Jeorje was heavier, and wise to her tricks. She punched at him, but with warded glass plates sewn into the lining of his jacket, the blows hurt her more than him.

And all along, those iron fingers closed tighter and tighter. Had the sun set? Or was her vision going dark?

But then the grip loosened. Selia blinked, seeing Jeorje rear back in the flickering light of the fires. Brine Broadshoulders, his mangled jaw askew, had the ancient Watchman by one leg and the back of his coat. He lifted Jeorje off her and hurled him from the stage.

Selia coughed, looking out over the townsfolk, many still fighting, others fallen, illuminated in the firelight. The sky was dark, and the folk from Southwatch, battling the other militias a moment before, broke off from the fighting and began to vandalize the buildings around the square.

"Creator," Selia breathed. It wasn't just vandalism.

They were scarring the wards.

❧

"The wards!" Selia cried.

"Ay, what's this?!" Raddock demanded.

"The night will cleanse the sin from Town Square!" Jeorje roared. His Watchmen gave a cheer and raised their spears, but the Fishers and Marshes hesitated, looking back to their Speakers.

Jeph Bales had Mack Pasture in a headlock. He heaved, throwing the older man stumbling toward the Speaker for Fishing Hole. "This what you wanted? To tear the town in half so the demons could have us?"

"Ent," Coran Marsh said from behind the protective cover of Keven's spear and shield. "Din't want Selia speakin' for this town, but that don't mean we're in cahoots with demons." He turned to stare at Raddock.

Raddock drew himself up, eyes ablaze with reflected fire. "Ent. Only ever wanted for Fishers to get some rippin' respect."

"Threw in with the wrong lot for that," Meada said.

"There's no time for bickering!" Selia snapped. "We have to protect the wards."

Keven nodded, hopping down from the stage to take command of his men. Raddock took the steps, but even he scooped up a broken spear shaft to use as a club and put a hand around his mouth. "Fishers! Protect the wards! Anyone gets in the way, gut 'em!"

Selia slipped two fingers in her mouth and gave a shrill whistle. She leapt off the stage and the scattered men and women of her militia began to form around her as she waded into the fighting, Brine, Mack, and Jeph at her back.

Selia cracked a Watchman across the head with her spear shaft, knocking off his steel-rimmed hat and dropping him to the ground. Close up, she could see the mind wards on the brim had been scratched, breaking the lines.

Fighting together, Jeorje's fighters were forced to abandon their assault on the wards to defend themselves.

That was when the demons arrived.

₰

They swarmed into the square, the cobbled greatward marred past even the slightest utility. Reaps of field demons, lithesome and fast. Copses of wood demons, lumbering but strong as ancient goldwood trees. Flame demons dancing between the legs of great rock demons that shook the cobbles with every thunderous footfall. Flights of wind demons circling in the sky.

And there were others, corelings out of Jongleurs' tales, never before seen in the Brook. Cave demons—terrifying armored monstrosities that skittered on eight long legs as easily on sheer walls as flat ground.

Manie Cutter hacked the leg from one, but the cobbles beneath him heaved, and he was thrown from his feet as a worm the size of a mustang burst from the ground in a spray of stones and soil.

The corelings ignored the Watches entirely, but the others were attacked with ferocity and precision.

Selia had been leading fighters against corelings for a year now and had never seen the like. Demons were animals, like nightwolves. They bit and clawed wildly, attacking when they sensed weakness, and retreating when they sensed strength.

This was different.

Stam Tailor raised his shield to fend off a pair of field demons. One clawed the wards in predictable fashion, but Selia could see it was a feint, keeping Stam's arm high as the other ducked his spear and darted in, biting his shield arm and severing the leather strap. The shield fell askew, and it was all the opening the corelings needed to fall on him.

The wards burned into his leathers offered some protection, and Selia threw her spear, taking one of the field demons in the side as it lunged for Stam's unprotected throat. Stam scrambled frantically back, but one of the cave demons turned and sprayed him with liquid silk. The viscous fluid covered the wards and the demon's legs began spinning him like a spitted hog as it bound him in thread.

Cutters rushed forward to hack Stam free, but the stones exploded at their feet as another of the worm demons surfaced. They stumbled back, and there was no warning before wind demons fell upon them, skewering men on their talons and launching skyward with a savage beat of their wings. One of the men managed to put the pick end of his mattock through a wind demon's wing, but Selia did not know if he'd saved himself or quickened his demise as both dropped heavily from the sky to strike the cobbles.

The cave demon had slung Stam on its back and was carrying him off by the time Selia snatched up his broken shield and used it to bash in the head of the squirming field demon still impaled on her spear.

She tore the weapon free, seeing the demon tactics repeated throughout the square. Corelings were raiding the buildings where the wards had failed due to fire or sabotage. Where needed, they killed defenders, but most were simply carrying folk off—wrapped in silk, hauled into the sky, or knocked senseless. The great coreling worms sprayed inky mist that fouled wards and seemed to paralyze victims long enough for the demons to wind around them and drag them down into their tunnels.

Demons are swarmin'. Selia shuddered as she remembered Renna Tanner's words. *Buildin' hives, and they need live larders to feed the hatchling queens.*

Was there already a demon queen in Tibbet's Brook? If so, Selia didn't know what hope they had, but she was never one to give up without a fight. She slashed the broken strap from Stam's shield and threaded her belt through the eyes to replace it. It wasn't the familiar weight of her father's shield, but she felt whole again as she returned to the fray.

The town's defenders fully engaged by demons, the Watches returned to the work of breaking wards. Soon the square would be defenseless, and they would move to the outer boroughs. Would even daylight stop those firmly in the mind demon's sway?

The only safe space left was Hog's store. Security had crank bows and they were putting bolts into anyone—coreling or Watch—who drew too close.

"Retreat to the General Store!"

Fighters and bystanders alike followed Selia's command, rushing the building.

"Ay, Selia!" Hog cried from inside.

"Stuff it, Rusco!" Selia pointed her spear at the sound of his voice.

Hog did not reply, but he opened the doors to his tavern wide, letting folk flee to succor. He emerged moments later, his heavy, muscled frame clad in armor of warded glass, with a helm and round shield to match.

Hog didn't carry a spear, just a smith's hammer with a glittering silver head. A field demon leapt on him, but its claws found no purchase. There was a thunderclap of magic as he bashed its head in. One of the Watches fired at him with a hunting bow, but the arrow splintered off harmlessly. Hog pointed at the man with his hammer, and store security shot him down.

Nomi Fisher ran into the store, clutching a bloody hand to her head. A moment later, Selia saw her run by again.

It was all the warning she had before the mimic demon struck, whipping an arm that grew into a long tentacle, ridged like a rock demon's armor, into the stones at their feet. Selia and her militia instinctively raised shields against the spray of rock and mortar, and in that moment of blindness the demons rallied around the great coreling, striking the defenders with sprays of silk and paralyzing spit in addition to tooth and claw.

Selia and Lesa fought in practiced unison, guarding each other and creating openings for the other to strike. Lesa kicked a field demon onto its back, and Selia skewered it through the unarmored belly. Selia pinned one of the cave demons against a wardpost, and Lesa hacked off two of its legs and part of a third where they met the thorax.

But the coreling struck back, spraying silk in Lesa's face. She gave a muffled cry and stumbled away as Selia stabbed the demon between the pincers, her spear going into its mouth and bursting up through its skull between its rows of great black eyes.

Lesa had dropped her spear and shield, falling to her knees as she struggled to claw the silk from her nose and mouth. Selia saw she could not breathe.

Keeping her shield up, Selia dropped her spear and snatched the warded knife from Lesa's belt.

"Stop thrashing." Selia gripped Lesa by the chin and pierced the silk covering the young woman's mouth. The blade came away gummy and wet with blood, but Lesa drew a gasping breath.

"Cad see!" Nose still bound, Lesa's words were barely understandable. "Geddid off!"

The silk was stuck fast to hair and flesh. Removing it would be painful, likely to leave scars to last a lifetime, but there was nothing for it. Brine and his Cutters were holding the line with help from the militias from the Square and Boggin's Hill, but there were corelings everywhere, and they would sense her weakness.

"Deep breath and keep your eyes shut tight." Selia took

the back of Lesa's hair, bunched at the base of her helm, in one fist, and a handful of sticky silk in the other. Killing demons had left her energized, bursting with strength, and she tore the hardening web from Lesa's face.

Lesa's shriek was a knife in Selia's heart. Her face was dark with blood in the flickering firelight. Selia glanced down, seeing hair and bits of skin in the handful of silk.

Along with the mind-warded steel plate that had been riveted to Lesa's leather helm.

She looked up just as Lesa punched her in the face.

"What did you think?" Lesa demanded as Selia stumbled back from the blow. "That you could seduce me like that Southwatch skink, and this time it would turn out well?"

Selia tried to find her balance, but Lesa kicked one foot out from under her, and she barely caught herself on her arms before smashing her face on the cobbles.

Lesa gave her no time to recover, kicking her hard in the stomach and then dropping down onto Selia's back. She put a forearm under Selia's chin and pushed her head forward with the other hand. Selia struggled, but Lesa, too, was charged with magic, and had the advantage of leverage.

"Your love is a curse, Selia Barren," Lesa whispered. "Everyone you give it to is destroyed by it. Now I'll be food for the demons just like your precious Anjy."

The words filled Selia with rage, and she heaved, getting a foot under her and kicking hard against the cobbles, flipping them both onto their backs. Lesa lost a breath as she was bashed against the stone but she kept the hold, continuing to choke as she worked her ankles around Selia's thighs, immobilizing her.

Selia struck Lesa's unprotected sides with her elbows, feeling a rib break, but under the demon's control, Lesa seemed immune to the pain. Selia thrashed, opening a tiny gap in the hold. She slid her fingertips in, prising her way between arm and throat. Lesa tightened her grip, but she could do little else to stop it. Lesa was strong, but her strength was cold—calculated. Selia's, powered with rage, came with a burst of adrenaline.

Selia tasted blood in her mouth, teeth clenched as she strained, pushing the arm from her throat. She forced them apart, gasping a breath and redoubling her efforts. She would not abandon another to the demons. She would not abandon Tibbet's Brook to a coreling hive. She would not—she would *not*.

Selia worked her other hand into the hold, and suddenly Lesa released her with a kick that gave her time to roll to her feet. Selia rose shakily to meet her. "This ent you, Lesa. Felt the coreling in my mind, too. Real you is in there. Fight. Resist with all you've got."

"There is no resisting the prince." Jeorje came up on the other side of Selia.

"We've all lost." Lesa held up Selia's brookstone necklace, clutched in her thick leather glove. The heavy cord was broken, but the stones were knotted in place to maintain precise spacing. If she could get it back, she could fix—

The thought broke off as the demon struck her mind, shoving past her defenses. As before, the mind demon delved into her darkest memories—moments of shame, failure, humiliation, and weakness.

She'd failed Anjy and Renna, but she stood strong for

those women. There was meat for the demon in those memories, shame, but some pride, too. But then it found something even more delicious.

Marry me, Bil Square said all those years ago. *Ent no more place in the Brook for square boys than girls. Don't mean we have to be alone.*

And Selia, broken and tired, had agreed.

The town celebrated the match, and even the elders seemed satisfied. The whispers stopped. But Bil was no more interested in her body than she was in his. They fumbled awkwardly abed a few times, eyes closed, imagining Creator-knew-what as they tried to maintain the arousal necessary to complete the act and produce a child. It ended in failure as often as success, with nary a skipped flow to show for it. Soon they gave up entirely.

Bil began disappearing for hours, sometimes barely making it home by nightfall. Once he didn't come home at all, and Selia went to bed sick with worry. He returned the next morning without explanation, for what could he say? Selia never asked whom he was with, but they both knew she was no fool.

She didn't resent Bil seeking love, even if secret trysts were all he could find. But it stung when men sniggered at her back, forcing her to wonder if they'd lain with her husband.

Soon after, folk began to whisper again, this time the word that would haunt the rest of her life.

Barren.

Selia felt the demon savor the word, drinking it like chilled nectar. There was so much shame and self-loathing wrapped up in that word. So much despair. Power it could turn against her—and, through her, the town she Spoke for. How many folk had escaped the riot in the square, cowering behind succor and waiting for dawn? What would happen to them if their Speaker became the voice of evil?

Selia struggled against the mind demon's power, but her anger and rage fed the demon as well, and it only increased the pressure against her. She had seen in their last encounter that negative emotion was its food and drink.

But had her life truly been one of despair? It was woven into the tapestry of her life, but it was only part of the picture. Selia focused back on her marriage, calling up memories the coreling prince disdained. The way Bil had made her laugh and brought her tea after a long day. The warm quilts that filled their home, and the impeccable way he kept their house while she was carrying the worries of the town.

Bil had been a good husband. They spent over thirty years together, loving if not in love. When the cancer took him, she wept bitter tears—not for a wasted marriage, but for all they shared.

Selia felt the demon recoil slightly, and seized on the slackening of control. If her love was truly a curse, why did she keep finding it, again and again?

She thought of Deardra—not the betrayal, but the intimacies and confidences they had shared, exploring something forbidden in the hope that someone else could understand.

Again the demon squirmed in her mind, pulling away from the thoughts and trying to force her back into memories of shame.

But Selia was done being ashamed of who she was. Done regretting decisions she would not have made another way if she'd had the chance to make them over again. She focused instead on the breathless passion she'd shared with Anjy, the raw intensity of Lesa's loving. She thought of the countless times she'd been there for the folk of Tibbet's Brook, solving problems from petty squabbles to coreling massacres. She'd lived a life to be proud of, no matter what Jeorje Watch or the demon prince might want her to think.

The demon was retreating from her mind now, unprepared for the force of her will, the intensity of positive memory and emotion she used like spear and shield in this psychic battle.

Its will fled her body, but Selia latched on to it, riding like a tether into the coreling prince's own mind. She sensed its panic as it tried to shake loose her mental hold, but the demon was controlling too many drones to fight her off. Through it, she could sense every mind—human and coreling—it was connected to, and in so doing she was able to sense its position.

The demon was right there in the square, just a few feet away. It was hidden behind a veil of magic, but she could see it now, with her mind if not her eyes. It was small, barely five feet tall, with an enormous head, slender limbs, and long, almost delicate talons.

One by one, the connections in the demon's mind winked out, demons and folk under its control regaining their senses as the coreling prince sought to focus its will on her. Selia saw into its thoughts in that moment, saw the web of caves on Mack Pasture's land where the captured folk were being held for the coming of the queen. It wasn't too late for them.

But it might be too late for her. With every drone the demon released, its will grew in strength, becoming a hillside—a mountain. The demon wrested control of her, seizing her mind in its mental talons and slowly crushing it, savoring her dawning realization that she was going to lose this battle.

I will tear open your skull and feast on your mind, its thoughts promised.

But then the blade end of Jeorje's cane burst from the demon's chest. Lesa came in next, punching its bulbous head with warded gauntlets.

There was an instant of freedom as the coreling prince reeled from the blows, but Selia knew it would not last; knew even these grievous injuries would not be enough to end such a powerful demon. She scrambled, snatching up the brookstone necklace Lesa had dropped. The moment her hands clutched the stones, etched with lacquered mind wards, the demon was shut out of her head.

Not so, Jeorje and Lesa. They stiffened as the demon returned its attention to them, but Selia gave it no chance, cracking the necklace across the coreling's face like a lash. The wards flared to life as they struck, again breaking the demon's concentration.

Jeorje shook off the demon's control again, yanking his cane free to bash the demon's knobbed cranium with the impact-warded head. Lesa continued to hammer it with punches as Selia whipped the necklace around the demon's throat and pulled tight.

The coreling raised a talon, drawing a ward in the air that flung the others back, but Selia had the cord wrapped around her fists and kept the hold, dropping to try and pull the demon down.

Instead the prince of demons swelled, growing as big as a wood demon. Selia was dragged upward, feet dangling in midair, the cord digging painfully into her hands, even as its wards flared brighter and brighter. The coreling's talons cut deep into her flesh as every demon in the square raced their way, desperate to protect their master.

But they were too late, as Jeorje and Lesa rushed back in. Lesa put her spear into the demon's heart, and Jeorje drove the spearhead of his cane into the coreling prince's skull.

The coreling gave a strangled cry, echoed in the shrieks of every demon in the vicinity. The prince collapsed, and a shock wave seemed to pass through the other corelings, wracking their bodies and leaving them curled up like dead flies on a windowsill.

Suddenly the square was quiet, save for the crackle of flames and the moans of the wounded.

Jeorje got to his feet, turning to Selia. He still clutched his cane, spear tip sizzling with power as it dripped black ichor.

Selia straightened. She had no armor or weapon, and the others were too far away to reach her in time if he struck.

And she was tired.

"Still think I'm a burden on this town?"

Jeorje locked stares with her, twisting the cane in his hands. "Always thought you were touched by the Core."

"You've felt that touch personally, now," Selia said. "Demon make you want to kiss another man?"

Jeorje scowled, but he lowered his cane. "Ent saying I forgive you for Anjy."

Selia put her hands on her hips. "Ent saying I forgive you, either."

"Ay, fair and true. But I never wanted . . ." Jeorje swept his hand over the square, littered with bodies of demon and folk alike.

"None of us did," Selia agreed. "That was the demon

talking. We stand together now, put out the fires and rescue the folk trapped in that hive, maybe we forget today ever happened."

Jeorje glanced at the stage. "Did you cheat the vote?"

Selia met his eyes when he looked back to her. "No."

"Ay." Hog came over to them, his armor spattered with blood and ichor, but a sheepish look on his face. "That was me. Selia didn't have anything to do with it."

"Corespawn you, Rusco!" Selia snapped.

Rusco shrugged. "You went down, Speaker, knew he'd come for me next."

"Ent wrong about that," Jeorje said. "But it doesn't matter. Coreling played us like a fiddle. Sent me looking for trouble, and would have found a way to start it, vote or no."

Jeorje's eyes flicked to Lesa, face bloody but still beautiful to Selia's eyes. "That going to continue?"

Selia crossed her arms. "Ay."

"Sure as the sun rises," Lesa agreed.

"Still don't approve."

"Don't care," Selia said.

Jeorje nodded. "Then let's put things back the way they were."

"No," Selia said. "High time we started making things better."

About the Author

PETER V. BRETT is the bestselling author of the Demon Cycle series—including *The Warded Man, The Desert Spear, The Daylight War, The Skull Throne*, and *The Core*—which has sold nearly three million copies in twenty-six languages worldwide. He spends too much time on the internet, but occasionally unplugs to practice kickboxing and dad fu. He lives in Manhattan.